MacBog's Revenge

By

Donald Corr

Illustrations by Donald Corr
Cover illustration by Frances Corr

Published in 2008 by YouWriteOn.com

Copyright © Text Donald M Corr

First Edition

The author asserts the moral right under the Copyright, Designs and Patents Act 1988 to be identified as the author of this work.

All Rights reserved. No part of this publication may be reproduced, stored in a retrieval system, or transmitted, in any form or by any means without the prior written consent of the author, nor be otherwise circulated in any form of binding or cover other than that in which it is published and without a similar condition being imposed on the subsequent purchaser.

Published by YouWriteOn.com

CHAPTER 1

"Steady!" growled the Major.

In the tense silence the men could hear their hearts thumping, breath rasping. Their bodies pressed against the ground, but they still felt the wind's chill caress as it came whispering and sighing through the sparse tufts of bleached grass. Above them in the steel-blue sky, so high as to be almost invisible, a pair of buzzards squealed and tumbled, oblivious to the drama unfolding below.

"Steady ... !"

They heard the first faint, ominous drumming.

"Hold it!" hissed the Major. "Wait ... for ... the ... order!"

The drumming grew louder. Suddenly a terrible unearthly howling rent the air and a swarm of black figures burst over the skyline.

The guns cracked and banged, sending a hail of lead whistling across the hillside towards the rushing horde. At least one body crashed to the ground, and a ragged cheer went up from the men behind the guns.

"Hold your fire" roared the Major, as the cluster of figures raced along the crest of the hill and out of sight. As though attached by an invisible string, another figure bobbed along some distance behind them. He appeared to be gesticulating. Barely audible, carried on the gusting breeze, faint shouts could be heard:

"Not so fast ... you little ... sheep-shaggers ... slow ... down ... you ... BASTARDS!"

This figure also disappeared over the hill.

Minutes slowly passed. The men waited, guns poised, nerves taut.

"Brace yourselves" shouted the Major. "Here they come!"

Once more they heard the distant drumming of feet on hard ground. Again the group of shrieking figures burst over the skyline. Again the guns cracked, and the men cheered hoarsely as another two appeared to fall, before the swarm of bodies thundered over the brow of the hill and disappeared from view once more.

The Major climbed stiffly to his feet and blew a long blast on his whistle. The men began to relax, tension easing away. They scrambled to their feet, stretching and laughing and slapping each other on the back.

"Well done, you chaps!" barked the Major. "Good work! Looks like you bagged three of the buggers on the first outing. Bloody good show!"

CHAPTER 2

Major Manley-Buttocks had two large balls of which he was inordinately proud - they were often the first thing guests remarked on when they arrived at Glendruel House, home of the Major, his wife Maud, and their daughter Cynthia. The balls were carved from finest Aberdeen granite, polished to a deep lustre and mounted on a pair of imposing stone pillars at the entrance to the estate. The gravel drive which swept between them curved up through an avenue of ancient Scots pines and opened out to give a splendid view of the shooting lodge. It sat in a hollow, protected by low, dark hills, a rambling, ivy-clad building in mock baronial style, encircled by an expanse of neat lawn and great banks of rhododendrons.

An unremarkable product of English shire society, the youthful Manley-Buttocks had undergone the normal progression from pea-shooter to catapult, air rifle to shotgun. On reaching maturity, and wishing to continue to indulge his enthusiasm for sending lead speeding through the air towards other life-forms, he decided upon a career in the army. He lied about his weight and obtained a commission in the Berkshire Light Infantry. After a long and uneventful military service he left the army and, on the proceeds of a generous gratuity and some inherited wealth, purchased the Highland sporting estate of Glendruel, where he spent several golden, gunpowder-scented summers assisting his paying guests to blast birds out of the sky. Never was a man more content.

The story would have ended here, had it not been for the terrible effects of Endemic Toe Rot which, like a devastating plague, suddenly swept through the grouse population of northern Scotland.

Endemic Toe Rot. Experts argued and many theories were advanced: some claimed it was spread by a new virus, some maintained that it was the result of changing weather patterns, others blamed pollution. The infection was not in itself fatal, but it had the effect of impairing the circulation in the birds' legs and eventually caused their feet to atrophy. They could still take off, but on coming in to land they tended to pitch forward and either break their necks or sustain brain damage. Soon the highland hillsides were littered with the bodies of dead grouse, their withered legs pointing forlornly skywards, their necks bent at unnatural angles, while around them their brain-damaged compatriots stumped crazily in ever-decreasing circles. Within two years the population of *lagopus scoticus*, the red grouse, was almost extinct.

For those landowners in the Highlands who were economically dependent on the grouse, Toe Rot spelled disaster. For years many of the great estates had been barely profitable, and now they faced bankruptcy. Many shooting lodges fell into disrepair. Windblown slates lay where they fell, paint flaked, and once-manicured lawns slowly surrendered to Nature's insidious advance. Rusting Land Rovers lay abandoned, weeds growing around their axles, tattered canvas flapping in the breeze. Over the estates a brooding silence hung heavily, disturbed only by flurries of bickering among the colonies of jackdaws, bright-eyed opportunists who had taken up residence in the crumbling chimney stacks. All over the Highlands ex-gamekeepers in fading tweeds sat slumped in the corners of bars, staring morosely into their glasses and reflecting sadly on the glorious days; days when the sky was dark with whirring wings, when whisky ran like water, and when the tips from grateful guests came in large, folding denominations. Now, a terrible blight lay across the land.

Several landowners tried desperate measures. One estate experimented briefly with radio-controlled grouse. Its gamekeepers were given short courses of instruction in the operation of the dummy birds. Strips of grass on the hillsides were mowed and rolled, and squadrons of model grouse would lurch and bounce along on their little wheels, painted balsa wings flapping manically until they struggled into the air. This idea was short-lived however. The occasional thrill of blowing one out of the sky with a fluke shot did not compensate the guests for the lack of realism as the 'grouse' rocketed vertically into the air, plunged Stuka-like to earth, or slewed across the sky in a series of loops and rolls while grim-faced keepers wrestled with the unfamiliar controls.

Another estate tried converting the firing apparatus used for clay pigeon shooting so that it catapulted stuffed grouse into the sky. This idea was also doomed to failure. The birds cartwheeled through the air in a very unrealistic manner and, as they followed an almost identical trajectory every time they were fired, the shooters soon got their sights in and hardly ever missed. In no time at all the stuffed grouse had been so patched and stitched together that they were utterly unrecognisable as birds.

Major Manley-Buttocks' flash of inspiration, however, had been truly brilliant in its simplicity. There were no grouse left to shoot at - so why not shoot the grouse-beaters instead? This would give continued employment to the beaters, who would otherwise be thrown out of work, and it would provide an exciting alternative for those wealthy guests who could only be persuaded to part with large sums of money in exchange for live targets.

Before Toe Rot had decimated the grouse, the beaters had been employed to march over the hills waving sticks and flags in order to flush the birds from cover and drive them towards the waiting guns. The beaters were mostly an unlikely assortment of university students, augmenting their grants, and unemployed youths from Scotland's cities, Glasgow in particular, who made the annual trip north for ready cash and a change of beer.

The Major realised that, before the beaters could be used as moving targets, certain precautions would necessarily have to be taken in order to keep casualties to an acceptable limit, as any adverse publicity could have a serious effect on what was potentially a very lucrative scheme. In return for a doubling of their wages, the beaters were obliged to sign disclaimers in the event of suffering any injuries in the course of their employment, and an unofficial code of practice was agreed on. Plastic safety goggles could be worn, thick clothing was allowed, and only light shot was to be used in the cartridges. The beaters would run an agreed distance away from the shooters and only two runs would be completed on any given day since, after a couple of charges across the face of the guns, the beaters would begin to tire (and, the Major reasoned, offer less sport). To preserve the idea of the traditional shooting season they would only be employed for a couple of months in the autumn, as they had previously been as grouse-beaters. Apart from keeping them fresh and fit, and lessening the chance of 'accidents', this limited availability of the shooting would increase its attractiveness to the clients. With all these safeguards, serious injury could be avoided, but the wealthy guests would still have the thrill of shooting at live targets which yelped and fell over when hit.

All went well for a while. Word of the novel form of sport available at Glendruel soon spread among the shooting fraternity, and the estate had no shortage of bookings. The Major's only problem was in attracting the right calibre of beater. There was a high drop-out rate and, even among those who lasted the whole season, there were the malingerers and the faint-hearted who persisted in running out of range of the guns, or dropping into the nearest hole and lying low till the shoot was over. The students were particularly hard to please and tended to whine when they were shot. One, whose father was a High Court judge, even threatened litigation and a national newspaper exposé after receiving a minor flesh wound. Buying him off with an envelope full of ten pound notes was the last straw for the Major, and he determined from then on that estate policy would be to employ only Glaswegians.

The Glaswegians were tough, impervious to wind and rain and, far from complaining, seemed to take a perverse pleasure in running through heather and being shot at. Before long a hard core of these beaters had evolved. At the end of each summer they would emerge from the bleak housing estates where most of them lived and, bidding farewell to familiar things - the smell of the kebab take-away, the distant howling of Rottweilers and Alsatians, the evocative sound of the wind whistling among the satellite dishes and the happy cries of muggers plying their trade - they would assemble at the railway station and board the north-bound train with the prospect ahead of two months of fresh air, excitement, and disposable income.

They were a motley collection - tall, short, fat, thin, and combinations of all these - a ragged-trousered, uncombed, gap-toothed, cross-eyed, leering, shuffling, nose-picking, bottom-scratching, farting rabble, many with features and limbs bearing the old scars from lead shot. When they congregated in any number they had a natural tendency to form into a tight huddle, like some many-legged beast. This behaviour had evolved as a result of running over hills and being shot at - it was a form of self-protection whereby the unfortunates on the periphery got hit while their fellows on the inside escaped, and kept warm as well. In spite of such apparently selfish behaviour, they regarded themselves as brothers-in-arms, united in the face of adversity, and they took a fierce professional pride in their occupation. They were The Beaters. And the Head Beater was Willie MacBog.

CHAPTER 3

"Get yer arses in gear, you snivellin' wee scumbags!"

Grallocher had once been the Major's head gamekeeper. Now, to his disgust, his title was 'Shooting Manager'. The demise of the grouse and the disintegration of the old traditional ways had hit Grallocher hard. His whole world had been turned upside down. Always a dark, taciturn man, now bitterness and resentment had come creeping into his soul. The only certainty left in his life was the Beaters. He hated them. To him they symbolised everything about the new order which he despised.

"Get into the trailer, you torn-faced little bastards!" he roared.

"Good man, that Grallocher" muttered the Major. "Bloody good man. MacBog! Let's have the damage report then."

"No' too bad, sur. Couple o' wee flesh wounds an' a twistit ankle."

"Very well; carry on, MacBog."

Willie turned and walked back to the trailer, hauling himself in beside the Beaters. Grallocher climbed into the Land Rover, slammed the door and, with a bone-jarring jolt, they set off along the rough track which led back to the lodge.

"Ye fuckin' basturd, Grallocher" screamed a Beater, as one of the wheels of the trailer crashed into a pot-hole. The Beater had been trying to light a cigarette, and the sudden lurch had caused him to burn the end of his nose. Grallocher smiled grimly. He always drove with the window open, the better to hear the cries of anguish from his tightly-packed cargo. His foot pressed harder on the accelerator - there was another pot-hole coming up.

The Land Rover ground to a halt beside a long, low, corrugated iron building. The Beaters clambered stiffly from the trailer, grumbling and rubbing their aching limbs.

"Moanin' wee pansies" muttered Grallocher. Perhaps the greatest cause of his resentment was that he was forbidden to lay a finger on the Beaters. On several occasions he had come close to physical confrontation with Willie, but he knew it was more than his job was worth. Willie's position as spokesman for the Beaters was tacitly accepted by the Major. Good Beaters who knew the ropes, and who were willing to take the money and keep their mouths shut, were hard to come by. Willie controlled them, maintained discipline of a sort and, most important of all, ensured that they delivered a sporting performance for the guests.

Willie was not a thing of beauty. Tall and thin, his pockmarked face was framed by lank, dark hair from which two monkey-like ears protruded. A spark of malicious humour flickered in his deep-set eyes, and when his face occasionally cracked in a smile it showed his few remaining teeth to good advantage. He wore a large pair of hob-nailed boots, a pair of torn and incredibly filthy trousers and a totally shapeless jersey which his mother had knitted from two different kinds of wool. After its first and only wash, the arms had shrunk but the main part of the jersey had stretched until it hung almost to his knees. From the shortened arms protruded thin wrists and two huge bony hands, which made sharp and sudden contact with the Beaters' heads on a daily basis. However, this caused no ill-feeling - Willie was the Boss.

The Beaters shuffled into the tin shed, the Bothy, their home for the duration of the season. It was furnished with a long row of metal-framed army surplus bunk beds, a couple of tables and a selection of rickety chairs and, at the far end, an ancient stove over which an assortment of damp socks and some nondescript items of underwear steamed gently. Their unusual grey colour and several obvious stains indicated that the washing instructions had been treated as loose guidelines rather than as actual directions.

Looking rather incongruous in such drab surroundings, a glossy array of well-formed ladies wearing only perfect sun tans pouted seductively down at the bedraggled degenerates milling beneath them. At this moment, however, the Beaters were far too tired to be affected by the visual allure of the tacked-up sirens. They threw themselves groaning onto their bunks.

The three casualties of the afternoon's shoot were not sufficiently injured to merit the attention of the local doctor, so Willie administered first aid. The Beater with the twisted ankle had it bound tightly with an old strip of bandage and was prescribed a day off work. Then Willie approached the other two, who lay apprehensively on their bunks.

"I demand a priest!" one of them shouted, as Willie produced his Swiss army pen-knife and selected the blade normally used for removing stones from horses' hooves.

"Cut the fucker's leg off" advised an unkind soul. Willie pinned the patient down and in a matter of seconds prised out the pellets which had penetrated the skin and splashed iodine over the wound ...

"Jesus fucking Christ!" the patient roared. Willie gave him a stinging slap on the ear. One of the spectating Beaters nodded, with a knowledgeable air:

"See that? That's alternative medicine" he announced to his companions. "Ah seen it oan the box, wan o' they docimentrys. When Willie thumps the boy oan the heid, he forgets all aboot his sair leg."

The patient was moaning and clutching his ear.

"See that! Ah tellt ye!"

Willie was putting the final touches to the last patient when Grallocher poked his head round the Bothy door.

"MacBog!" he snapped. "The Major wants to see you in his office. Now!"

"Away an' stick yer heid up yer arse" muttered Willie, without looking up. He smoothed a strip of elastoplast over the patient's leg.

"OK. Yir cured. Keep yer weight off it an' no sex fur a week."

The Beater nodded warily, conscious of the threat of alternative medicine.

"Right boys, get yersels tidied up. Ah'll go an' see whit the old basturd's wantin'."

He set off across the drive to the front of the house and strode in, hob-nailed boots clattering on the wooden floor. Several guests standing in the hall turned and stared. He rattled his knuckles on the office door, and marched in.

"Ah! MacBog!"

"Sur."

"An errand for you MacBog. My little gel's arriving home today from that damned finishing school. Bloody nonsense! Bloody expensive too! Wife insisted, you know. 'Etiquette and manners'. Waste of time and bloody money. Hrrumph! Anyway, point is, the gel's coming back for the season, wife's idea, put her in charge of the guests' cuisine. Time she did something useful. Grallocher's otherwise engaged, MacBog, so take the vehicle and get down to Inverdruel smartish. Train's due at six-thirty. Chop chop!"

"Sur."

With a suddenly heavy heart Willie turned and left the Major's office. He went round to the side of the lodge and climbed into the Land Rover, put it into gear and rumbled slowly off down the gravel drive. As he passed between the Major's balls and out onto the main track he reflected morosely on Cynthia's visits of previous years. The Major's daughter was a snot-nosed little shit. Always complaining, always whining: the Beaters smelled; the Beaters called her bad words; the Beaters peed in the bushes; the Beaters took their trousers down and pointed their bottoms at her. Jesus Christ! Willie sighed and shook his head sadly. He could do without it.

Inverdruel village came into sight. It lay in a valley, surrounded by low hills. Peat smoke from the evening fires spread in horizontal wreaths, giving it a sleepy, timeless appearance. There was a central square with a hotel, a post office and a couple of shops, and several streets of small stone cottages. Beyond the houses a squat, granite church sat on a slight rise, and to one side of the village was the small railway station. Willie drove up and parked behind it. The train had not yet arrived, so he wandered onto the platform and took a seat on the edge of the big tractor tyre which the station-master had painted white and filled with flowers. Before long the train came chugging into view. With a squeal of brakes it drew in to the platform and juddered to a halt. Doors slammed open, and the passengers began to alight.

There were several bright-eyed hillwalkers clad in gaudy anoraks and festooned with ropes and rucksacks, and a tired gaggle of local women, back from a day's shopping in the big town, laden down with bulging bags and chocolate-streaked children. But no sign of Cynthia.

"Where the f ... " thought Willie. Then he saw her.

Gone was the buck-toothed, gum-chewing runt of previous years - a beautiful, glowing, gazelle-like creature descended from the carriage.

" ... Cynthia?"

"Why, hello Willie" she breathed. "How are things at the Big House? How are Mummy and Daddy?"

"No' too bad" stammered Willie, caught completely off guard. "The old bugger's still givin' us ... a hard ... time."

His voice trailed away.

"Forthright as ever, Willie", she laughed, a delicate, tinkling laugh, which sent electric tremors down Willie's spine.

"Christ Almighty" he thought, "what a wee doll!"

He loaded her cases into the back of the Land Rover and hauled himself in behind the wheel. He sneaked a furtive glance across at Cynthia. The pigtails, the crumpled school uniform were gone - instead, he saw neatly bobbed hair, slender thighs encased in tight denim, and the air was filled with the faint but pervasive smell of expensive perfume.

Willie shook his head. "What a wee doll" he thought, as he crashed the gears and set the Land Rover in motion. "What a wee doll!"

They headed out of Inverdruel, turned off the main road and began the bouncing, lurching climb up the steep track which led towards the estate. As they crested the hill and started the long descent into Glendruel the sun was setting behind them. Gnarled pines glowed a deep orange in the weak light and far below, in the dark bowl of the glen, a thin, peat-black ribbon of water snaked along. Dotted across the far hillside the remains of long-abandoned farms mouldered into the boggy ground, rushes growing thickly where there had once been pasture. The gaping doorways of the ruined buildings now let in sheep which had come like maggots to infest the remains. Dark windows stared like empty eye sockets, reflecting no light. From a distant tree plantation the harsh bark of a dog fox echoed, and the sound seemed to hang in the chill air.

Cynthia shivered. She had never liked this place. The signs of past habitation only made it seem more desolate. But, in the warmth of the Land Rover, with the lights winking on the dashboard, hearing the familiar growl of the engine, and with Willie at the wheel, she felt safe. She glanced across at Willie. He was bent over the wheel, staring ahead, concentrating on the pot-holes in the road. She saw the pitted face, the lank hair, the broken, dirty finger-nails, and she felt strangely moved.

They climbed back into the sunlight again, leaving behind the melancholy, deserted valley. Then they rounded the final bend, and Glendruel House lay before them.

CHAPTER 4

Willie stuck his head round the door of the Bothy. It was deserted.

"Tea-time" he thought. "Thank God for that; ah could eat a scabby dug withoot cutlery."

Built onto the rear of the lodge, a solid stone out-house which had originally served as a cool-room for hanging grouse had since been converted into the Beaters' kitchen and canteen, thus ensuring their strict segregation from the paying Guests. Willie ducked and threw open the low door.

Inside was a scene of near-Dickensian squalor. Apart from a single bulb which dangled from the ceiling, the long room was lit only by the grey light which filtered through a tiny, cobwebbed pane of glass high in one corner. The bare stone walls were stained with mould and grime, and a rough wooden table stretched the length of the stone-flagged floor. Ranged on benches along either side sat the Beaters, spoons poised in anticipation. The only table decoration was a huge bottle, its neck barnacled with a thick crust of ancient tomato sauce. The Beaters liked their tomato sauce, and applied it liberally to most dishes. At the far end of the room stood a massive cast iron cauldron, with a firebox beneath it which occasionally threw out a flickering orange light. Beside the steaming urn stood Cook.

"Aye, Cook - whit's fur tea the night?" shouted Willie, as he clumped across and took his place at the table. Cook pretended to extract a fat forefinger from her nostril and study it closely.

"Looks like mince."

"Aw, c'mon Cook, don't keep us in suspense!"

"Keep the heid, Willie, keep the heid! Right lads, on the menu tonight we have ... wait for it! ... Biff ... estoofad ... d'Avignon!"

A thunderous tumult arose from the Beaters. They cheered, they roared, they rattled their spoons on the table, they drummed their boots on the floor in an ear-numbing cacophony of approval. Cook held up her hands with a blushing display of modesty.

"With Turnip Fricassée ... "

This performance was repeated every night, with Cook making ever more extravagant claims to culinary sophistication. The names which she plucked at random from an old cookery book bore no resemblance whatsoever to the contents of the steaming urn.

The evening meal was always basically the same - great lumps of stew and potatoes and, Cook's pièce de résistance, doughballs. Doughballs which bobbed and jostled in the cauldron like a herd of albino hippopotami frisking in a mud-hole. Doughballs of such a sublime density that only their backs showed above the surface of the bubbling stew. Doughballs which, when smothered in tomato sauce, reduced the Beaters to a state of dribbling ecstasy.

Cook was of generous build, with twinkly blue eyes and a ruddy, weather-beaten face jammed into a mop of frizzy grey hair. She wore voluminous dungarees, and the sleeves of her thick woolly jersey were rolled back to reveal brawny forearms covered in tattoos of mermaids, anchors and other nautical paraphernalia. She had spent seventeen years on a Hull trawler, working as ship's cook, until one day the crew had discovered that she was a woman and put her ashore at the next port of call, which happened to be Aberdeen. Women, of course, are notorious bringers of bad luck to fishermen.

She had turned up at Inverdruel Highland Games, competing in the heavy events, when the vacancy for General Housekeeper and Beaters' Cook was brought to her attention. She was the only applicant for the post, so Major Manley-Buttocks hired her, and she had since made the position her own. (The trawler she had been working aboard ran onto a sandbank on its way back to Hull and was completely wrecked).

As the scalpel is to the surgeon and the brush to the artist, so had the massive iron cauldron become the symbol of Cook's calling. She had spotted it lying, rusting, in a scrapyard outside Aberdeen on one of her shopping trips to the abattoir. It had originally been part of the tryworks - the great pot into which chunks of blubber were tossed to be rendered down into oil - on an old Norwegian whaling ship. A fossilised crust of blackened blubber still clung to its rim, and this imparted a peculiarly oleaginous flavour to some of Cook's more delicate creations, but not a single complaint was ever heard from the devoted band of gourmets who, even now, sat, spoons poised, waiting for their Biff estoofad d'Avignon ... with Turnip Fricassée.

CHAPTER 5

"Rise and shine, boys, rise and shine!"

Willie battered a saucepan against the iron stove.

"C'moan! Get yer arses in gear!"

A dull chorus of muttering and groaning arose from the shapeless mounds on the beds.

"C'moan ye lazy wee shites - UP!"

Tousled, disorientated heads poked out, staring uncomprehendingly through sleep-gummed eyes.

"Get up, ye wee basturds!"

Like primeval life-forms emerging from long hibernation the bleary figures slowly crawled from under their blankets, yawning and stretching and scratching absent-mindedly at their private parts. Again the deafening clangour from the saucepan assailed their eardrums, and they scuttled, pale and shivering in their grimy underwear, to form a line at the door of the washroom.

The grass sparkled in the morning sunlight with a coating of frosty dew, and the Beaters were glad of the warmth in the canteen as they clattered in and took their places at the long table. The fire crackled cheerily and Cook was bent over her cauldron, swaying and undulating like an elephant at a disco, as she plied a wooden paddle to and fro in the thick, bubbling porridge.

Ranged along the table were the extra ingredients which the Beaters liked to add - sugar, treacle, jam, syrup. Some of them thought they could also detect traces of the previous evening's Biff in their porridge, but they kept quiet about it - no point in upsetting Cook.

When they were finally bloated to bursting point with the porridge and huge mugs of tea, the Beaters straggled round to the front of the lodge, and clambered into their trailer. They huddled together in a tightly packed mass, the subdued hum of conversation interspersed with the gentle sound of breaking wind and the rasp of matches being struck. Soon a blue haze of cigarette smoke hung above their heads in the crisp morning air.

"Whit's keepin' the basturds?"

"They'll still be haulin' up their fur drawers."

"Naw - they're probably still wipin' their botties."

"Aye, that's a job ye cannae hurry. Nuthin' worse than sittin' oan a hill aw day wi' keech in yer cleft."

The imposing main door of the lodge swung open, and the Guests began to emerge.

Three spotlessly clean and shiny Land Rovers were drawn up in front of the House, waiting to transport the Guests and their accoutrements to the hill. They stood around, their chattering punctuated by outbursts of raucous laughter, while Grallocher loaded hampers, guns, shooting-sticks and all the assorted baggage required for a day's sport.

"Ye gaun yer holidays, Grallocher?"

The Beaters chuckled.

"Mind an' send us a postcard, eh!"

"Aye, wan wi' naked wimmen oan it."

"Wi' big tits!"

A small muscle on the side of Grallocher's face twitched.

In years gone by, the shooting estates' clientele had been composed largely of the English upper classes, but nowadays the Guests were far more cosmopolitan. In fact, of the present party, only one, Tarquin Ross-Pettle, was truly of the English aristocracy. He came from a long line of Ross-Pettles and had the soft, pink cheeks, crimped blonde hair and languorous manner which betrayed centuries of careful in-breeding. When he roared through Inverdruel in his open-topped vintage sports car, immaculate in blazer and cravat, more than one middle-aged female heart missed a beat.

Standing beside him, and engaging him in an animated but rather one-sided conversation, was Sidney Blatch. Sidney had only recently taken up shooting, but he had compensated for lack of experience by making free with his cheque book in gun shops and sports outfitters all over London. Everything he wore was spanking new and the finest that money could buy. He was a small, round, jolly man, who would have sold his grandmother to white slavers if it had been a cash-only deal. His expression of genial bonhomie never altered - he even wore it in his sleep - but whenever a deal was in the offing his eyes would narrow alarmingly. Years in the used-car trade had made Sidney a wealthy man, and he had recently decided to purchase the lifestyle to match. Just at this moment, he was making a vain attempt to do a deal on Tarquin Ross-Pettle's vintage roadster. He had tried blandishments, he had tried offering used notes - he had even tried narrowing his eyes alarmingly - but all to no avail.

"Toffee-nosed git" thought Sidney bitterly. "Tight-arsed, toffee-nosed bahstard." He knew a club-owner in Streatham who would have paid through the nose for that particular model. His train of thought was suddenly interrupted by a loud squeal from Mrs Grossburger, the American guest.

"Ah jest lerv the way yew Uro-peeyans tawk! Ah cain't unnerstan' a ward yew'r sayin', but ah thank it's REAL sexy!"

Dolly Grossburger, rich widow of the recently-deceased owner of a chain of fast-food joints, had been brainwashed by countless hours of soap operas into believing that all Europeans had noble blood and lived in castles. She had flown over to get one.

At the moment she had three in close attendance - Ferdy Ploppwaft, a German horse-breeder; Henri Piptraud, owner of a small French vineyard; and Tomas Grobbelwoenck, a Dutch pig-farmer. None of them had a castle.

Dolly squealed again, and tossed her expensively-permed mane of bright blonde hair, which tumbled around her chubby, thickly-powdered cheeks. Sidney scowled at her. After a lifetime of transforming old, worn-out cars into superficially viable models, he could tell an old banger when he saw one.

"Bet 'er chassis's knackered" he thought, with a cruel smile.

"'Er big end's definitely gawrn!"

Yes. Dolly had been disappointed at the lack of success with her latest bottom-tuck. She was thinking seriously of changing her cosmetic surgeon on her return to the States.

"Hot dawg! Yew Uro-peeyans'r sich pahrfit gen'le-men, yew c'd teach them ole rednecks back home a thang'r two!" shrieked Dolly, as Henri gallantly assisted her to heave her bulk into the leading Land Rover, his hand sliding perilously close to her rump. Ferdy and Tomas watched closely. Henri was already leading the field - and setting a fast pace.

The convoy set off, the Guests' vehicles leading the way, Grallocher and his cargo of Beaters bouncing along in their wake, a thin blue vapour trail of cigarette smoke swirling in the slipstream. They lurched and yawed along the rough track, occasionally descending into frost hollows, when the morning stillness was rent by a wheezing, rasping cacophony as the keen air bit deep into the moist recesses of the Beaters' lungs, displacing the previous night's warm residue.

The track led finally onto a flat hill-top. Dotted across the uneven ground was a row of butts - excavated hollows surrounded by low walls of turf where, in the days of the grouse, the shooters would conceal themselves from the approaching birds. There was no need for concealment now, but they still provided useful shelter from the biting wind which always seemed to blow on these high tops.

As the Guests climbed out of the Land Rovers there was a tingle of anticipation - damn it all, this was what they had paid good money for! They were clad in the de rigueur uniform of waxed cotton jackets, tweed caps, 'plus four' trousers, thick woollen stockings and stout brogues. All except Mrs Grossburger, who was squeezed into an expensively-cut suede jacket, a pair of large, but still figure-hugging, white pants and high-heeled, intricately-tooled cowboy boots. There was a chorus of excited chatter and much brandishing of hip flasks while Grallocher unloaded the food hampers and the Major allocated guns and cartridges. The Guests positioned themselves along the line, two to each shooting-butt.

"Good Lord!"

Tarquin Ross-Pettle gave an involuntary start as he turned and found himself staring into the round, jolly face of Sidney

Blatch, who immediately narrowed his eyes alarmingly. Sidney was not a man to give in easily.

"Fancy that, Tarky" he chortled, "you'n me sharin' an 'ole, eh! Wot a lark!"

Ross-Pettle shuddered and looked away.

Ferdy Ploppwaft and Tomas Grobbelwoenck also had cause for alarm. From their butt they could hear the delighted shrieks of Mrs Grossburger as Henri gave her a hands-on demonstration of how to hold a gun.

Preparations complete, Grallocher climbed into his Land Rover and rumbled off over the hill.

The Beaters were huddled behind their unhitched trailer, sheltering from the wind, when Grallocher roared up.

"Right, you shit-faced little bedwetters, let's be having some action!"

Resignedly, the Beaters got to their feet and pulled on their safety goggles.

"MacBog! Don't let the bastards run too fast, and keep them close to the guns!"

"Aye, aye, Grallocher, keep yer hair oan - ah know the score."

"OK, boys" shouted Willie. "You heard the man. Get yersels sorted oot."

Elbowing and jostling, the Beaters squashed into a tight huddle behind Willie.

"Right lads, on the count o' three, go like fuck! One ... two ... three"

They were off!

Legs pumping, lungs straining, they sprinted up the low rise which took them out onto the open hill-top in full view of the shooters. There were a few seconds of frozen silence as they crested the rise, hearing only their own rasping breath and thudding footsteps. Then, suddenly, BANG, BANG ... BANG; pellets began to whine past them. They ran, aiming for a point on the horizon, cursing, panting, splashing through pools of stagnant water, stumbling over tussocks, screaming and roaring in a mixture of blind panic and pure exhilaration as the pellets whistled around them.

In what seemed like seconds, but was in reality a couple of minutes, they were across the open ground and staggered, breathless and shaking, into a grassy hollow where they threw themselves down. In the distance a whistle shrilled.

"Jee-zus Christ!"

"Ah'm gettin' too old fur this - ah'm knackered!"

"Someb'dy ... push ... a fag."

"Shut yer mouths a minute!" roared Willie. "Any o' youse basturds get peppered?"

They looked around. They all seemed to be accounted for, and no-one had been hit.

"A clean sweep, eh!"

"Those silly basturds, they couldnae shoot shit oaf an elephant's arse!"

They were still cheerfully swapping obscenities when Grallocher appeared, purple and breathless, at the edge of the hollow.

"Aye, ah thought you little turds would be happy" he panted. "Not one o' you got hit, eh, and you'll be expectin' wages I suppose! Bugger me!"

"No thanks", said Willie. "An' ye've nuthin' to complain aboot - we kept the right distance. It's no' oor fault if they bawheids cannae shoot."

"It's maybe your fault for lettin' your wee pals here run too fast" muttered Grallocher.

"Can ah help it if the boys are finely honed athletes?" asked Willie, a picture of injured innocence. "Runnin'-machines at the height o' their powers? Brought to a peak o' perfection by long years o' rigorous trainin' an' total abstinence from drink an' wimmen?"

Grallocher sat down heavily on the bank, glaring at the Beaters, who wore their finest choirboys' smiles.

It was time for the next run. Once more they crowded into a huddle behind Willie, donned their goggles and, on the order, set off on the mad scamper over the hill, howling and roaring as they tripped and tumbled across the face of the guns. They were almost out of range when there was a dull THWACK, and one of the Beaters crashed to the ground, clutching his thigh. The others kept running until they had reached cover, where they threw themselves down, wheezing and gasping. The shot Beater came limping in behind them, ignoring an outburst of sarcastic applause and emphatically turning down several offers of the kiss of life and a request for his boots in the event of amputation. He hauled himself into the trailer, where he sat, inspecting his wound and muttering darkly.

On the far side of the hill, the Guests relaxed with chilled wine, cold chicken, paté foie gras and other assorted delicacies. But there was a discordant note to their chatter, and their conversation became muted as Major Manley-Buttocks approached. He could not help but notice this, and he had the unpleasant feeling that trouble was brewing.

CHAPTER 6

From its shelf high on the mahogany-panelled wall the stuffed wildcat snarled, lips drawn back in a permanent rictus, at the moth-eaten old stag's head, which squinted back impudently with its offset glass eye. In the room below the crackling flames of the log fire were reflected a myriad times in the lead crystal decanter and the cut glass whisky tumblers set out on the low table.

"Vee shod hobble dem wit ropes - maybe dat wod do the trick ... " suggested Ploppwaft, his long, heavy-jawed face never changing its expression of lugubrious solemnity.

"Nein, nein, Ferdy!" interrupted Grobbelwoenck, a malicious glint in his piggy eyes. "How about we fill der pockets wit big stones? DAT wod slow de liddel boggers down, eh!"

"Wha not jest fill the sonsabitches fulla licker?" squealed Mrs Grossburger. "Shore as hell'd cramp their stahl!"

"Très bien, très bien, ma petite!" cried Henri, in a voice thick with emotion. He patted Dolly's well-rounded knee. "Tu es magnifique!"

Sidney Blatch shook his head.

"'Ave to be scientific abaht it, 'avn't you? Dope! That's wot you need. A blahdy great eiperdermic raht up their arses! It works wiff 'orses, don't it?"

"I can't STAND cruelty to animals" snapped Tarquin Ross-Pettle. Sidney glared back at him; then all eyes turned as the door opened and the Major entered the room. Before they could say a word, he held up his hands in a placatory gesture.

"I know, I know. Let me assure you, I do understand. Every sympathy, every sympathy ... "

"Look here, Major," interrupted Ross-Pettle "why on earth can't we just use heavier shot, knock more of the blighters over?"

There was a general growl of approval from the guests.

"Understand your feelings, old man, understand your feelings ENTIRELY! Greatest sympathy. Can't promise anything. BUT - I'll speak to MacBog in the morning, see what we can fix up, eh? - a word in his ear, y'know."

The Major backed slowly out of the room, and pulled the door quietly closed behind him.

Dammit!" he thought. "Damn and blast!"

He had these problems before: Guests complaining of lack of sport. You had to tread such a bloody fine line, that was the trouble. Shoot too many Beaters, and they go all bolshie on you. Can't afford to upset MacBog either. Little buggers'd run over broken glass for MacBog, dammit!

"Talking to yourself, dear? A bad sign, you know."

"Ah! Maud, m'dear. Yes, yes - slight problem with the Guests. Sort it out in the morning."

"Good show. Well, don't let me hold you back", and she gave a low, throaty chuckle.

"The old trout's in unusually good form tonight" thought the Major, as he watched his spouse trundle along the corridor, humming cheerfully to herself. "A definite spring in her step. Hmmmm."

When Willie arrived in the canteen the Beaters were already making inroads into large plates of 'Biff en dob Marseillaise'. He took his place at the table.

"Lads are a bit quiet tonight" he thought. He had expected them to be in good form after coming back from the hill relatively unscathed. Glancing down the table, he noticed that one of them had pushed aside his plate, untouched.

"What the hell's the matter wi' you?" he enquired.

The Beater said nothing, and stared at the floor. There was silence. One of the others cleared his throat, and spoke ...

"The Beast almost got him."

"You poor basturd" Willie said. "Under the circumstances, ah'm sure Cook'll no' mind if ye cannae manage yer grub."

The Beater nodded his head, ignoring the hand which immediately snaked out and appropriated his plate.

'The Beast' was a reference to the Major's wife. Maud Manley-Buttocks was a short woman, with a powerful, stocky build. She was respectably conservative in appearance - tweed skirt, deerstalker hat, sensible woolly stockings and a pair of polished brogues with a tread which made the standard policeman's boot look like a dancing pump, but from behind her thick spectacles a pair of small eyes gleamed with an almost manic intensity. Maud Manley-Buttocks was possessed of unusually strong natural urges, which the Major usually managed to avoid by sleeping in a separate bedroom with a double lock and a chair wedged firmly under the door handle.

Mrs Manley-Buttocks had a habit of wandering the grounds, just as darkness was falling. In spite of her solid build, she had the unnerving ability to move with cat-like stealth. The Beaters would sometimes sense they were being watched and occasionally caught the sinister glint of her spectacles in the half light, as she glided silently among the rhododendrons.

Over the years, there had been a couple of incidents where a Beater had strolled out of sight of his fellows and apparently vanished. Muffled shouts had been heard and the sound of thrashing in the undergrowth, then, after a short silence, an exultant and unearthly cry of "Geronimo!" Shortly afterwards the victim had burst forth from the shrubbery, dishevelled, ashen-faced and trembling. None of the victims would speak of their experience, but they never went near the rhododendrons again.

"You huv the day off the morn", Willie told the distraught Beater "an' ah'll get you some tins o' beer."

Next morning, Willie stood in the Major's office, where he had been summoned. On the desk between them lay a fat brown envelope. The Major leaned forward and prodded it towards Willie.

"Let's say it's a, um - a bonus" he said, indicating the envelope with a podgy finger.

"What for, sur?"

"It's the Guests, MacBog. They want to use heavier shot. I'm sure you do understand the situation?"

He smiled warily, and leaned forward again, sliding the envelope closer to Willie ...

"Fifty pounds in there, MacBog."

"It's no use, sur. The boys'll no' do it. They'll end up hospital cases."

The Major's eyes flashed with anger, but he controlled his temper.

"One hundred, then."

"Ah telt ye sur, the boys'll no' do it."

The Major's voice rose querulously. A purple blotch appeared on each cheek.

"They'll damn' well do it if you tell them to!"

"Aye, but ah'm no goin' to tell them!"

The Major glared at Willie.

"Don't be a bloody fool, man. Just take the money and shut up."

"No, sur."

"Hell's bells, MacBog, they're Beaters, not bloody ballet dancers!"

He scraped back his chair, and leaned over the desk.

"God almighty!", he roared "if there are no Guests your damned Beaters will be out of a bloody job!"

For several seconds they stared at each other.

"A deal" said Willie. "No way you're usin' heavy shot ... "

The Major started to go purple again. Willie held up his hand.

"Listen" he said. "Ah'll see if the boys'll go a wee bit closer to the guns, OK? That's it. That's yer lot."

"But the Guests ... "

The Major slumped back in his chair. He knew it was the only concession he was going to get.

"AND", continued Willie "ah'll take this fifty quid. For compensation."

"Compensation?" said the Major, glancing up sharply.

"Aye, compensation. For the Beater that got the fright o' his life in the grounds last night. Be around the time yer missis was oot for her stroll?"

The Major looked puzzled. Then his expression changed to one of slow comprehension. His eyes bulged, and he pointed a quivering finger at the door ...

"Out, MacBog!" he roared. "Get out!"

The Beaters were assembling outside the kitchen when Grallocher strode past. His face was contorted with strange muscular spasms - he was smiling!

"Hope you scumbags have plenty bandages. You'll be needing them!"

"Away an' fling shite at yersel" muttered Willie.

Grallocher strode off, an evil smirk still playing about his features.

"Whit's up wi' that smarmy arsehole?" enquired one of the Beaters, wiping porridge from his face with a filthy sleeve.

"Bad news" said Willie. "If those basturds had their way you'd be blindfolded and chained together. We've got to go in a wee bit closer, boys, keep the Major sweet. Seems the Guests urnae happy."

"Ach, no problem, Willie."

"Aye, no bother tae us."

But Willie knew the Beaters were none too pleased at the prospect. With the light shot that was used and the distance they were allowed to keep from the guns, incapacitating injury was very rare; but going closer would start to increase the odds in the shooters' favour.

They crossed the hill that day howling like dervishes as the pellets hissed and buzzed around them. By the end of the second run there were four casualties, including Willie, who had been nicked on the skull by a pellet.

Afterwards the Major called Willie over in a voice booming with geniality, as though the morning's conversation had never taken place.

"Looks like you've been in the wars, MacBog!"

"Sur."

"You'll be glad to hear the Guests were very pleased today. Just thought you'd like to know."

"Ah'm delighted for them sur. Give them somethin' tae put oan their postcards."

"No need for sarcasm, MacBog. Not in front of the Guests, eh? What's the damage then?"

"Four. Three's no' too bad, but one's got pellets in a bit deeper. Doctor job, ah think. So wan o' yer Guests can put a notch oan his gun ... sur."

"Yes, yes, MacBog. There'll be a small bonus for the injured party, and we'll get McLush up to have a look at him. Carry on, then."

The Major turned to rejoin the Guests, who were boisterously proposing toasts. Through the general sound of merry-making Ross-Pettle's plaintive tones could be heard:

"For the last time Blatch, no, I will NOT sell you my motor car."

On their arrival back at the Lodge, the Beaters set about manhandling their stricken comrade from the trailer. He was groaning terribly, and insisted that beer, cigarettes and a woman be brought immediately, before death overtook him. The Major marched across from the House.

"Stop that damned snivelling, man!" he barked. "Get a grip on yourself!"

The Beater muttered weakly that self-abuse was the last thing on his mind.

"I've telephoned Doctor McLush" announced the Major "and he'll be here shortly to patch you up. Meantime, I'll send my daughter over with the first aid box for the rest of you. Carry on", and he turned on his heel and scrunched back to the House to attend to the Guests.

A couple of minutes later Cynthia emerged from the main door. The Beaters stared as she approached.

"She's a wee stoater, eh!"

"Ah wouldnae mind a lumber wi' that! If she asked me nicely, that is!"

"God, aye. Ah'd let hur experiment oan ma body fur a fiver."

"Wan mair word" Willie said quietly "an' yous'll be shittin' teeth fur a week."

The Beaters fell silent, though some of them gave Willie a funny look. At one time or another most of the Beaters had encounters with the local belles in Inverdruel, but Cynthia was ... something else.

Apparently oblivious to the primitives' rapt attentions, Cynthia strode into their midst, placed the first aid box on the back of the trailer, and opened it up. "All right" she said brightly, "bring me the wounded." The Beaters lined up to have their injuries attended to. Finally, Willie stepped forward. He stared down at Cynthia as she dabbed away the smears of dried blood.

"Ah think she fancies you, Willie" sniggered one of the Beaters. Cynthia said nothing, concentrating on the job in hand, but her cheeks betrayed the slightest hint of a flush. She carefully applied a plaster.

"Thanks, doll" Willie said. "Worth gettin' shot fur!"

As some of the Beaters put their fingers down their throats and made retching sounds, Cynthia swept the first aid equipment into the box, snapped it shut, and half walked, half ran back to the lodge.

A happy grin spread across Willie's face. He turned and absent-mindedly smacked the nearest Beater across the head, but it was only an instinctive gesture, for his mind was obviously elsewhere.

The Beaters were still standing around the trailer, smoking and chatting, when a distant rattling became apparent, growing louder by the second. Through the trees a battered Morris Minor could be seen, screaming up the drive in the wrong gear and trailing a thick plume of blue smoke.

"It's the Doctor!" shouted one of the Beaters, as the ancient vehicle swerved erratically towards them and braked to a halt, spraying them with a shower of gravel, "an' look, boys, fur Chris'sake, look - he's got Jim with him!"

The Beaters burst into a chorus of cheering, raucous laughter. There was indeed another figure, sitting hunched in the passenger seat.

With some difficulty, the Doctor climbed out of the car. He was a small, slight man, wearing a shapeless tweed coat which was several sizes too large for him. His mane of wispy white hair was matched by an unkempt moustache, and his nose and cheeks had that bright crimson flush often seen on a well-smacked bottom.

"Wher's the payshen?" he demanded.

"Right beside you, Doc. The one that's lyin' on the ground bleedin'!"

"Aye, if you're quick you'll maybe save him yet."

The Doctor bent over and peered at the injured Beater, who was propped against the wheel of the trailer, still making impossible demands.

"Come on lads" shouted one of the Beaters, "let's go an' say hello to Jim."

They raced over to the car and clustered round the passenger window.

"How's it goin', Jim ma boy?"

"Gawd Almighty, look at the state o' him!"

"When'd ye last huv a bath, Jim?"

"Look at his coat - it's filthy!"

With an expression of utter melancholy, Jim looked out reproachfully at the circle of hooting, jeering faces. At that moment the Doctor turned from his patient and shouted over -

"Bring ma bag, Jim."

One of the Beaters held open the car door, and Jim climbed stiffly out and limped over, the Doctor's medical bag gripped between his teeth.

"Thasha good boy" said the Doctor, and patted Jim on the head. He immediately threw himself onto his back. The Doctor scratched his stomach.

"Asha good boy, asha good boy."

When he had finished scratching the matted hair on Jim's stomach, Doctor McLush turned his attention once more to the groaning patient. Rummaging through his bag he produced a huge syringe, which was already filled with a clear liquid.

"Thish'll hurt, laddie" he said, "but don' you worry - isha pain-killer."

The Beaters winced and looked away as the Doctor held the hypodermic high above his head, before his arm described an arc through the air and descended with a thud on the patient's leg.

There was silence for several seconds, then a blood-curdling, nerve-piercing scream, which reverberated around the courtyard, then echoed back from the surrounding hills.

"You'll be right as shixpensh in a coupla minitsh, laddie" muttered the Doctor, raking once more through the jumble of implements, bottles and medical paraphernalia in his bag. Finally, with a cry of triumph, he pulled out a pair of long, thin forceps.

"Aha! Got you, you little bashtards!"

"Doctor McLush! So glad you could make it old boy. How is the patient? Not malingering, I hope?"

"G'day, Maze-yor, g'day. Payshen's doin' fine. 'Spec full r'covry. Need coupla days to coop'rate. Gave'm shum penshillin - sh'd do ... trick."

"Good show, Doctor, frightfully decent ... little, er, something ... for your trouble", and the Major passed over the clinking parcel, which the Doctor immediately clasped protectively to his bosom. He bent towards the Major, putting his finger to his lips conspiratorially.

"Mus' dash, Maze-yor. 'Mergincy. Took farm'r's wife'sh blood preshor yes'day - left bloody rubb'r tube - tied round'r arm. Mus' dash!" And he turned and, with just a hint of unsteadiness, headed towards his car.

Jim, who all this time had been lying on his back in the vain hope that somebody else might want to scratch his stomach, rolled over and limped after his master, attended closely by a thick cloud of fleas who knew that if Jim got too far ahead they would be homeless. With some difficulty the Doctor wedged himself behind the wheel, slammed the door and roared off in a spray of gravel, still in the wrong gear.

"Well" said one of the Beaters, looking down at the groaning patient, "he'll no' be goin' dancin' tonight!"

CHAPTER 7

The atmosphere in the Bothy hummed with suppressed excitement. Saturday night! Inverdruel Hotel! Drink! Wimmin! Singin'! Dancin'! A scrum of Beaters jockeyed for position in front of the broken shard of mirror propped against the wall in the washroom.

"Ooooh! Yah sexy beast!"

"Slacken aff yer stays, girls!"

"Come an' get me, baby!"

Ancient, gap-toothed combs were flourished with all the panache of a conductor's baton. Clean underpants, "Ye never know yer luck", were hauled over scrawny buttocks. After-shave lotion from a colourful assortment of bottles with labels trumpeting names like 'Brute', 'Macho' and 'Conquistador' was splashed about liberally. Great dollops of gel were worked into hair, and forelocks twisted and teased into sensuous curls. God help the wimmin! Those Beaters who still had teeth scrubbed them furiously, crooning lines from popular love songs through mouthfuls of toothpaste.

There was the sudden roar of an engine, and the squeal of brakes outside.

"It's the bus, boys! All aboard!"

Last-minute panic, the final primp, check the money, check the flies, the mad stampede onto the bus. Christ, Saturday night, bloody great!

"What a bunch o' fuckin' pansies" jeered Grallocher. "A spot o' National Service - that's what you bastards need!"

"Jist shut yer mouth and drive, Grallocher" shouted Willie. "Are youse all here?"

There was a great roar of "AYE!", and the bus lurched off. As the ancient single-decker slowly picked up speed and rumbled away down the drive the echoes from an exuberant chorus of "Hey ho! Hey ho! It's off to work we go!" hung in the still evening air.

Every Saturday night the Major laid on this trip to Inverdruel for the Beaters. It was the part of his job that

Grallocher hated most. He had to crank up the old bus and drive the little bastards all the way to the village, just so they could piss away their wages in the bar of the hotel. Grallocher himself did not touch drink - he regarded the taking of alcohol as teetering dangerously close to pleasure. While the Beaters caroused he would sit in the bus, reading over his favourite passages from 'Mein Kampf'.

As a swarm of bees is unerringly drawn towards the sweetest flowers, so the rusty charabanc with its fragrant cargo of matinee idols rattled and bounced inexorably closer to the pheromone-flushed females of Inverdruel.

"We work all day and get no pay, hey ho, hey ho, hey ho, hey ho!"

Grallocher's knuckles whitened on the steering wheel. Oh, how he hated the little bastards!

Groaning and straining, the ancient engine hauled the bus over the top of the final hill and there, spread below them, like Rome before the Huns, lay Inverdruel village.

The bus trundled along the main street, turned in to the square and ground to a halt outside the hotel.

The Beaters tumbled from the bus and jostled noisily into the public bar of the Inverdruel Hotel, sucking in great, invigorating lungfuls of thick, smoky air. Ahhh ... lovely! All week they had been looking forward to this. The local belles were out in force and their strongly-scented perfume mingled with the Beaters' 'Conquistador' to produce a potentially explosive mixture.

The bar was dimly lit, but the atmosphere was warm and inviting. In a small alcove a log fire crackled cheerfully, and round it several of the Guests from the Lodge were comfortably ensconced, savouring expensive malts.

Like a sparrow on a fence post, the Oldest Inhabitant perched on her stool at the far end of the counter, peering intently at the taut buttocks of the two crimson-faced snooker players who were doing battle on a badly-adjusted television set behind the bar. As her favourite potted the winning ball she cackled and punched the air with a gnarled fist.

From a room off the main bar came the staccato click of pool balls and the thunk, thunk of darts hitting a board, the whole punctuated by expletives and raucous laughter. Doctor McLush lurched unsteadily across the room, muttering to himself, a length of rubber tube trailing from his jacket pocket. Over in the corner, tethered to a table leg with a piece of knotted string, sat Jim, gazing beseechingly at anyone who passed by. Someone had given him a bag of prawn cocktail flavoured crisps, his favourites, but the bag had got jammed over his nose. He realised that he looked ridiculous.

As Willie elbowed his way to the counter there was a squeal of delight from the barmaid, Andromeda. Andromeda had the sort of figure that would have had Rubens reaching for his chequebook. She and Willie had a long-term but easy-going relationship, based on uncomplicated lust. The Beaters whistled and jeered and called for buckets of cold water as she came round from the bar, crushed Willie to her ample bosom and planted a big, wet kiss on his stubbly cheek.

"Ach, stop it, Andromeda" he protested, "no' in front o' the boys!"

"Ah cannae help it, it's ma hormones, they're goin' berserk."

She released Willie from her powerful grip.

"Hang on a minute Willie, an' ah'll get you a pint, ah'll jist serve this gentleman first", and she turned back to the bar, where Sidney Blatch was clicking his fingers vigorously.

"Could I 'ave a whisky, luv, an'" he dropped his voice to a conspiratorial whisper "a large double for my ... associate ... 'ere", indicating Tarquin Ross-Pettle, who sat hunched over the bar, his head clasped tightly in both hands.

Under the euphoric influence of several pints the Beaters began to feel as good as they knew they looked. Like ducklings making their first sorties away from their mother in pike-infested water they edged cautiously away from the bar and began to eye up the local damsels, who had formed a defensive ring at one end of the room. Before long, shrieks could be heard as the more audacious Beaters put out feelers, and soon they were jostling at the bar ordering Harvey Wallbangers, Screwdrivers, Pink Ladies and Snowballs - the defences had been breached!

Other defences, too, were being breeched. Above the clamour of bar noise snatches of conversation could be heard:

" ... ma petite, ma 'art, eet goes ... boom ... "

"A real Dook! Whaddya know!"

"Ma sharmeeng, petite ... ma cherie ... "

Then a piercing trill cut through the hubbub. Glasses were held, poised in mid air. Mouthfuls of beer remained unswallowed. In the frozen silence the rumble and clunk of a ball slowly making its way through the innards of the pool table sounded unnaturally loud. Every eye was fixed on the bar, where Dolly held outstretched a plump hand, one podgy finger adorned by a massive, glittering diamond.

"You ole houn' dawg!"

Henri Piptraud blushed and looked coyly at his feet. Dolly was not to know that he carried half-a-dozen condoms and a spare engagement ring in his top pocket at all times.

The rest of her words were drowned in a thunderous outburst of shouting, cheering and whistling from the Beaters, who sensed a free drink. Dolly had turned to the bar and was holding out the finger with the sparkling stone for Andromeda's inspection.

"... an' he's ree-lated to a real lav Dook! ... lives in a li'l ole sha-teau near Paris, France ..."

From the end of the bar Ferdy Ploppwaft and Tomas Grobbelwoenck glared sourly across at their rival. Then Grobbelwoenck bent over and, covering his mouth with his hand, began to whisper earnestly in Ploppwaft's ear. Ploppwaft stared along the bar in the direction of Henri, and a malicious smile slowly spread over his doleful features ...

Suddenly a young man pushed his way through the throng of interested onlookers. He wore a trilby and, jammed in the hat-band, a piece of white card proclaimed 'PRESS' in felt-tipped capitals. Scoop McCronnicle, trainee reporter with the Inverdruel Bugle, the local news-sheet, had spotted a story. In his endless quest for a headline, Scoop often had to perform minor miracles with the scant material available:

"TURNIP PRICE RISE SENSATION!" and "INVERDRUEL TRAIN LATE - EXCLUSIVE!" were two of his recent efforts.

In a brief, no-nonsense manner he whipped a notebook from his back pocket, licked the pencil stub which he produced from behind his ear and stared at the happy couple expectantly. He realised that he was probably on to the biggest social splash since Queen Victoria's train had stopped for several minutes at Inverdruel Station towards the end of the nineteenth century.

Henri stared at Scoop.

"No comment!" he hissed. "No comment!"

But no-one noticed. Dolly was unstoppable. Scoop's pencil became a blur as he noted details of guest lists, number of bridesmaids, length of bridal train, number of layers on wedding cake ...

Henri wilted visibly, his eyes became glazed, inside him something died. Just like the prospects of the quiet, registry office wedding he had in mind.

Dolly finally came to a breathless halt. Scoop snapped shut his notebook and elbowed his way off through the crowd and out of the bar. He leapt into his Reliant three-wheeler which was parked outside and, jamming his foot hard on the accelerator, puttered off in the direction of the Inverdruel Bugle office.

In his mind's eye he could see it already, screaming from the hoarding outside the newsagent:

"BURGER WIDOW TO WED WINE BOSS - EXCLUSIVE!"

Suddenly, there was a commotion over in one corner, and a buzz of anticipation went through the room. The band had arrived.

Cases and boxes were hauled in through the fire door at the back of the bar, and the artistes began positioning amplifiers, assembling microphones, untying knots in electric cables and taping up bare wires, all the while giving four-letter ripostes to the cheerful hecklers in the watching crowd. For this was no ordinary band. These musicians were the flag-bearers of heavy rock in the North, veterans of countless late-night sessions, legends in their own time. They had been a small-time dance band until Inverdruel was connected to the National Grid in the 1950s when, overnight, they became a small-time electric dance band. It had taken several decades, but they had built up a reputation as a gutsy, no-nonsense, hard-drinking, hard-playing outfit. They were the best band for miles around. They were the only band for miles around. They were ... The Inverdruel Rockettes!

Their lead singer had a sallow complexion and dark eyes. After a lot of practice in front of his bedroom mirror he had managed to get his eyes to smoulder. The women loved it. He had neatly-trimmed sideburns and a prominent quiff. The women loved that too. His stick-thin legs were encased in tight drainpipe trousers, and he wore a black leather jacket which bore the legend 'Elvis Lives' in peeling, self-adhesive letters. His real name was Duncan McGlumpher, but he preferred to be called Troy Fontana. He had been lead singer with The Inverdruel Rockettes for seventeen years but, just to be on the safe side, he still kept on his day job operating the Stop-Go sign for the local Roadworks Department.

His backing was supplied by a diminutive guitarist known as 'Flintstone', who drove the Roadworks Department truck. The rumours that he had to have blocks of wood lashed to the soles of his boots to enable him to reach the controls were completely untrue. The accordionist was the Roadworks

Department foreman. He was not the best accordion player in the world, but he WAS the Roadworks Department foreman.

Ringo Duff, on drums, was the wrong side of sixty. His sleeveless woollen pullover, humphy back and carpet slippers tended to detract from the menacing image the Rockettes tried to project, but he had the only set of drums in Inverdruel and also a basic knowledge of electricity. He claimed that the severe tremor in his hands was the result of years of virtuoso drumming - years of virtuoso drinking, muttered unkind souls.

A sudden drum roll and clash of cymbals attracted the attention of the milling crowd in the bar.

"Laydees 'n' Gen'l'men - a big hand please for your very own, The ... Inverdruel ... Rockettes!"

It was some time before the uproar finally subsided. When it did there was a slightly embarrassing silence because the accordionist was still struggling with his harness - so Troy did a bit of smouldering, to get the women warmed up, and Flintstone picked out a few speculative chords. Finally, with a brief wail from his instrument, the accordionist got himself untangled - and they were off!

To the uncalloused ear it may have sounded discordant, loud even, but the Beaters were galvanised - they bopped, they gyrated, they whirled and they pirouetted, hurling their screaming partners around the room as Ringo's drums thundered and the accordion squawked and amplified guitar chords crashed around their ears. And, interwoven through the wall of noise, Troy Fontana's nasal drawl told tales of hopeless love, of tragic car crashes, runaway husbands and dying sweethearts.

Then came Flintstone's moment of glory - his solo spot. The drums were stilled, the accordion lay unsqueezed, Troy Fontana stood back from the microphone, and Flintstone stepped into the glare of the spotlight. His stubby fingers began to flit up and down the fretboard, like animated sausages, as he tentatively picked out individual notes, slowly creating ever-more intricate patterns, quietly at first, then gradually building up speed, faster and faster, till the guitar wailed and cried like a living thing under his caressing fingers and, finally, the pièce de résistance, he started to play the guitar - with his teeth!

The crowd listened enthralled, overawed, as he plucked out a throbbing rock medley. Then suddenly, amplified by the microphone, there was a strange sound, a kind of TWANGaaaarrgh! - and Flintstone's teeth flew over the heads of the horrified audience. Also amplified by the microphone in the sudden silence was Troy Fontana's angry hiss:

"You stupid little shit - I warned you about those dentures!"

- and Flintstone's toothless reply,

"Pith off, McGlumpher, bloody know-all bathtard!"

While Flintstone set off to find his teeth, the rest of the band held a hurried conference, then announced that there would be a short interlude. This signalled a rush to the bar by the Beaters, terrified that their women's alcohol levels might drop - they had to keep the alcohol levels up to be in with a chance of romance later in the evening. Over in the corner Jim had finally managed to get the crisp bag off his head and was now lying under a table, chewing contentedly on Flintstone's dentures.

Fifteen minutes later Flintstone still had not found his teeth, and the crowd was getting restive, so Troy insisted that they start the second session. After much microphone tapping and some ear-splitting squeals from the amplifier, and after successfully extinguishing a small electrical fire, the band launched once more into the raunchy, no-holds-barred rock music for which they were justly famed. By now the musicians, as well as the audience, had quite a high alcohol content, and the dancing was, if anything, wilder than before. The floorboards vibrated under pounding feet, sweat ran in streams, women flew through the air, glasses rattled and bounced - and, picking his way through the melee, Doctor McLush slowly worked his way across the room towards the door marked 'Gents'; until he trod on a lump of chewed pink plastic and his foot shot from under him. He staggered sideways, arms flailing like windmills as he made frantic attempts to regain his balance. He crabbed across the dance floor, picking up speed as he went until, with an apocalyptic crash, he vanished into the middle of Ringo Duff's drum ensemble. A lone cymbal rolled across the floor between the legs of the stunned dancers.

Ringo staggered to his feet, white with fury.

"You old bastard" he yelled, "the only set of drums in Inverdruel. By God, you'll pay for this!"

Doctor McLush began to extricate himself from the heap of scrap where Ringo's drums had been.

"Air turbulensh ... mushda been pock't ... air turbulensh."

"You drunken old bastard" roared Ringo. "I've a bloody good mind to put you in hospital!"

"Don't do that, Ringo" someone shouted, "think of the patients!"

"Jeethuth Chritht!" screamed Flintstone, who had just noticed the chewed lump of pink plastic lying in the middle of the floor.

"My tceth! You bathtard, you fucking bathtard, look at the thtate of my teeth!"

"Turbulensh, mushda been turbulensh" mumbled the Doctor, trying to shake a side-drum off his foot.

A second intermission was announced and Doctor McLush continued unsteadily on his interrupted progress towards the door marked 'Gents'. Ringo frenziedly set about trying to construct something percussive from the wreckage of his ensemble, while Flintstone sat in the background, his head in his hands, muttering through clenched gums.

After a short interlude, the Rockettes struck up once more - they were hardened troupers and the show had to go on. The crowd sensed that some of the sparkle had gone out of their playing, but Ringo performed on his newly-assembled bongo section with a controlled fury which drew gasps of genuine admiration from the spectators.

After a couple of numbers the crowd began to get restless. Troy, deciding to end on a high note, sang one last tear-jerking, gut-wrenching ballad relating the emotions of a lonely country boy whose crippled true-love and her faithful old dog had died in a fire-ball after a head-on collision with a bus full of orphans as she was travelling to the county jail to pay her sweetheart a final visit before he went to the electric chair for a murder of which he was wrongly convicted. There could be no doubting the passion and emotion which Troy put into the song, but several people thought the bongo accompaniment struck a rather discordant note.

When the applause had died away, Troy stepped up to the microphone and announced that it was time for the Local Talent Spot.

The Beaters took part enthusiastically in these events. Between them they had a range of unexpected accomplishments and it also gave them an opportunity to impress the local females. As the Rockettes anxiously pulled microphones and electrical equipment out of his path, one of the Beaters clambered unsteadily up onto the low dais. After several unsuccessful attempts he finally managed a shaky handstand then, as beads of perspiration appeared on his brow, he shot one hand out at right angles, balancing precariously on the remaining hand. The crowd watched in silence as a pint of beer was conveyed across from the bar and his outstretched hand clamped round it. Then, twisting his head round horribly, he gulped down the beer, hardly spilling a drop. As the empty glass was removed he crumpled to the floor to a smattering of applause. Someone in the audience commented loudly;

"That basturd wid stick his heid up his own arse fur a free pint."

However, the disgruntled critic was probably just a less talented person.

The next artiste to step from the crowd was a diminutive Beater. He proffered a crumpled note to Troy Fontana. Troy reached for the microphone:

"Lay ... dees'n Gen'l'men, for our next act I give you ...

He stared with furrowed brow at the scrap of paper in his hand, before bending down to confer with the next act, who was beaming happily at the audience. Troy straightened up.

"Lay ... dees'n Gen'l'men, I give you ... Jimmy and his Jolly Juggling Gerbils!"

The crowd roared their approval as the small Beater extracted two squirming rodents from the depths of his jacket.

"Aw, that's a shame" came a female voice from the crowd.

"Aye, cruelty" added another.

"Let me tell you, madam" said the small Beater, puffing his chest out indignantly and staring steely-eyed at his accusers, "these are specially bred Himalayan Gerbils, so they're used to heights, see. An' what's more" he added, "safety precautions will be taken!"

And he held up for the audience's inspection two little helmets made from cut down ping pong balls, with thin pieces of coloured tape attached. He secured the helmets to the gerbils' heads with a neat bow tied under their chins.

"Music, maestro!"

To the accompaniment of a bongo roll the small Beater began to juggle with the gerbils. Faster and faster they whirled, spinning round and round, little arms and legs outstretched until, with a final flourish, the small Beater tossed them high in the air, pirouetted, and caught them again. Applause exploded across the room and he bowed theatrically, then held the gerbils aloft.

"See!" he cried triumphantly at the Animal Rights faction in the audience. "They enjoyed it!"

True enough, though their little sides were heaving like bellows, under their lop-sided helmets the gerbils' beady eyes seemed to gleam with excitement.

As the applause died away one of the Beaters shouted for Willie to give them 'Andromeda's Poem'. At the bar Andromeda was playfully chewing Willie's ear.

"We want Willie! We want Willie!" the Beaters chanted.

"By popular demand" announced Troy, "I give you, with ... "Andromeda's Poem", Willie Mac ... Bog!"

To enthusiastic encouragement from the Beaters Willie made his way to the microphone, bowed, cleared his throat and gave a wildly over-emotional rendering of the love-poem he had composed for Andromeda in their early courting days:

"Andromeda, ma heart's desire,
Ah wanna hug 'n' squeeze you,
Ah'd sook warm beer thru' sweaty socks
If that is what wid please you.
Andromeda, so sweet, so round,
You move with perfect grace -
You've rosy cheeks, a joy to see,
On either side o' yer face.
Andromeda, ma blood does bubble
When ah see yer curves an' angles,
When yer lips caress ma stubble
An' you squeeze the bit that dangles.
You make ma lovin' heart beat faster,
Ma one desire, ma Aphradite,
From tender bits ah'd rip a plaster
If ah could see you in yer nightie."

The Beaters cheered and howled and stamped. They stood on tables and whistled. They just loved a spot of culture. Above the noise nobody heard the shrieks and crashes as a bewildered-looking Doctor was hurled from the door marked 'Ladies'.

Then the lights were flashed on and off. The evening was drawing to a close, and the Rockettes struck up with their last number, a slow rendition of 'Save The Last Dance For Me'. The Beaters crowded onto the floor, propelling their paramours before them, and began to shuffle around with them in the half-light. Now that the bar was closed they could devote their whole attention to overwhelming their partners with the smouldering heat of their passion.

    Andromeda made her way through the throng, and locked Willie in a powerful embrace. Surfacing for breath, Willie was startled to find himself staring straight at Cynthia, as she sat alone in the alcove, watching. For a few seconds their eyes locked, then the surging crowd came between them ...

CHAPTER 8

The Bothy presented a scene of domestic tranquillity. One of the Beaters sat hunched over, absorbed in the task of glueing a patch over a hole in his trousers. If he had thought to take them off first they would not have become stuck to his leg, and he would have been spared the agony of having them ripped off by helpful comrades, leaving a large bald patch on his otherwise hairy limb.

The revellers who, whether by accident or by design, had missed the bus home the previous night, had now all turned up, footsore and bleary-eyed. They sat hunched around the glowing stove, hands and stockinged feet extended to the shimmering heat, boasting of their exploits. The weaker spirits, or perhaps those who had more to boast about, lay in their bunks groaning fitfully, their plaintive pleas for silence ignored by several Beaters who were exuberantly gambling with the paltry remains of their week's wages.

The toilet door hung open and a Beater crouched on the pan, brow furrowed in concentration as he perused a back copy of 'The Inverdruel Bugle' whose pulpy, absorbent paper was ideal for wiping bottoms. The only drawback was the poor-quality newsprint - often a Beater would dab at his nether parts with the 'Bugle', only to have 'EXCL SIVE!" or 'SH CK!' imprinted in huge black letters across his buttocks.

The weather was deteriorating fast, and the Bothy shook under sudden gusts of wind which cast rattling splatters of rain against its tin walls. From the window low clouds could be seen scudding along under a washed-out sky. But, with the stove going full blast the Beaters were snug and warm, they had the whole day to themselves, and Cook always made Spotted Dick and custard on Sundays.

Across in the Lodge the Guests slumped somnolently in the deep, soft armchairs scattered around the lounge, perusing the Sunday papers, sipping whisky, or just dozing in front of the blazing log fire. Tarquin Ross-Pettle toyed idly with the 'Times' crossword.

"'Ere, Tarky, mind if I borrow your pen 'arf a mo'?"

Grudgingly, Tarquin handed over his pen to the beaming Sidney, who proceeded to encircle several advertisements in the 'Exchange and Mart'.

"Couple o' real bargains 'ere" he muttered to himself, tucking the pen away in his inside pocket.

Henri and Dolly sat perched on the edge of the sofa in the big bay window, their knees just touching, her hands clasped tenderly in his. Henri was concentrating on gazing into her eyes - he knew that women appreciated these little touches. Suddenly, he tightened his grip on Dolly's plump digits.

"Merde!" he hissed under his breath.

"Married?" said Dolly uncertainly, then her face lit up.

"Wha, sure, Onree honey, jest's soon's we git settled in that li'l ole sha-teau. Ah thawt we hid that awl 'ranged, baby?"

"Oui, oui, ma petite, oui, oui"; the smile was fixed rigidly on Henri's face, which was more than could be said for the stone in Dolly's engagement ring, which had just come loose in his hand. He had had trouble with this ring before. An earlier and very promising relationship had come to an abrupt end when the same stone had plopped into a bowl of consommé just as Henri was in the act of proposing.

"Excusez moi un moment, ma cherie" he muttered, and rushed precipitately from the room.

"They're jest so darned impetuous, these French men, ain't that a fact!" squealed Dolly, looking round and smiling uncertainly at the other guests, who had observed the proceedings with some bewilderment.

"A touch of the trots, I'd say - what do you reckon, Tarky?" chortled Sidney. "No bowel control, these blahdy Frogs, that's their trouble."

"Yes, yes, Blatch" snapped Ross-Pettle testily from under the table, where he was searching in vain for his pen.

The Beater who had the bald patch on his leg took some consolation from the fact that he had managed to screw a fiver out of the Frog for a half-used tube of glue.

"The basturd's probably a sniffer - he wis bloody desperate" he told his envious associates, as he held the five-pound note up to the light.

CHAPTER 9

Henri raised Dolly's hand and brushed it gently with his lips. He delicately placed little kisses along her arm, but only as far as the elbow.

"Bonne nuit, ma cherie" he whispered as she backed slowly through the bedroom door. She held up her hand and twiddled her fingers.

"Naht, y'ole Cas'nova, yew!"

As the door was closing, he blew Dolly one final kiss. Henri was far too subtle a practitioner in the art of love to alarm his intended by any inopportune display of brutish behaviour. He turned and, with a light-hearted step, set off towards his own room. Two figures appeared at the far end of the hallway, coming towards him.

"Gute nacht, Henri" Ferdy Ploppwaft chuckled.

"Ja, you haf a goot sleep - MA PETITE!" sniggered Tomas.

Henri looked after them suspiciously as they proceeded along the corridor. As they passed out of sight down the stairway he heard Tomas mutter something, then Ploppwaft's high, whinnying laugh. He was overwhelmed by a sudden sense of foreboding. He knew that his conquest of Dolly had not endeared him to his rivals - but was it his fault that women found him unbearably attractive? Then he called to mind an episode that had occurred earlier in the day. He had broken off briefly from staring into Dolly's eyes - it began to hurt after a while -when his attention was drawn to Tomas and Ferdy sitting at a table in the corner of the lounge. They had their heads together, and Tomas was writing something on a piece of paper. When they realised that Henri was watching they immediately looked furtive. What had they been up to? Again, Henri felt a vague sense of foreboding.

He let himself into his room and absent-mindedly began to undress. He put his clothes away neatly and donned his silk monogrammed pyjamas. By the time he had completed his exercises, brushed his teeth and plucked a couple of stray hairs from his eyebrows, his disquiet concerning his fellow guests had begun to ease.

Outside, the storm continued to rage unabated, but his room was comfortably warm. The ancient central heating system, though it tended to rumble and clank intermittently throughout the night, was remarkably effective. Delicately stifling a yawn, Henri pulled back the starched linen sheet and climbed gratefully into his bed.

About the same time, in another part of the building, Maud Manley-Buttocks entered her own room. She almost failed to notice the small sheet of neatly-folded paper lying just inside the door. With a grunt, she bent down and picked it up. Opening the note she read:

"My darling,

I am mad with desire.

I must have you.

Come to my room tonight.

Henri"

Henri had almost dropped off to sleep when the door crashed open. Propping himself up on one elbow, he rubbed his eyes and squinted uncertainly at the stocky silhouette framed in the light from the hallway. A sudden silent flash of lightning bathed the room briefly in a garish light, and illuminated Maud Manley-Buttocks, clad in a crimson baby-doll nightie trimmed with fake fur and pom-poms. Behind her bifocals her eyes blazed with lust.

"Henri!" she rasped in a deep, gravelly voice. Henri's mouth opened and closed soundlessly.

" ... sacre bleu ... " he croaked, unbelievingly, as the door swung closed ...

The Beaters snored and twitched under their mounds of blankets, their sleep undisturbed by the fury of the storm. The wind funnelled through the glen and came hissing between the trees. It roared against the solid bulwark of Inverdruel House, spilling around and over it in great, swirling eddies. Broken twigs and small stones rattled against the tin walls of the Bothy and an empty dustbin spun away, clanging and booming, into the outer darkness. The rain had abated now, and the moon appeared intermittently in gaps between the ragged, scudding clouds, bathing the landscape in an eerie light.

Suddenly, every Beater was awake, nerves jangling. Through the tumult of the storm a long, terrible, blood-curdling scream had pierced the night. As its echoes died away the Beaters heard, above the buffeting wind, a hoarse cry of "Geronimo!"

CHAPTER 10

Although rain seeped steadily from the grey clouds which drifted slowly across the glen, the storm had largely blown itself out.

The Beaters had been hoping for a cancellation but the Major had consulted Grallocher, who advised strongly that the day's shooting should go ahead. He countered the Major's argument that the Guests might suffer some discomfort with his own suggestion that the wet conditions would slow the Beaters down and make them easier targets. Besides, the Guests would be leaving soon to make way for the next party, and he wanted to give them every opportunity to knock over a few more Beaters.

Grallocher sat in his Land Rover, sounding the horn impatiently. He stuck his head out of the window.

"Come on, you little bastards" he roared, "this isn't a holiday camp."

The Bothy door burst open and a line of Beaters marched out in single file.

"Hey ho! Hey ho! It's off to work we go!" they sang cheerfully, in time to their tramping feet. Clad in a mind-boggling assortment of oilskins, sou'westers, ancient cycling capes, decrepit raincoats and black plastic dustbin bags, they looked like a gang of marauding penguins setting off for a fancy-dress party.

"Jesus Christ!" muttered Grallocher, shaking his head, as his nostrils were assailed by the pungent odour of mildewed plastic and perished rubber. With much crackling and flapping, the Beaters piled into the trailer where they were soon hunched happily under a burgeoning cloud of cigarette smoke.

The Guests were assembling round their vehicles, but there seemed to be a spot of confusion. Henri Piptraud and Mrs Grossburger had failed to appear. The other Guests were beginning to get impatient, when Dolly came clicking down the steps in her cowboy boots. "Sorry, yew guys. It's Onree. He shore as hell is actin' weird."

It transpired that Dolly had gone up to Henri's room when he failed to appear for breakfast, and she had heard the sound of sobbing coming from behind his door. When she knocked and tried the handle there was a cry of "Non! Non!", and a heavy, scraping sound, as though he were pushing a wardrobe or some other heavy piece of furniture against the door. When she identified herself he seemed to calm down, but still refused point blank to leave his room.

"Ah thank" opined Dolly "Onree's a li'l bit hahly-strung, him bein' French 'n'all."

Ferdy turned and winked slyly at Tomas.

"Ma petite!" whispered Tomas out of the side of his mouth, and put up a hand to conceal a broad grin.

Minus Piptraud, the convoy set off from the Lodge. After the storm the track was partially flooded and the Beaters were alternately splattered with mud from the rear wheels of the Land Rover, then rinsed clean as they bumped and splashed through the pot-holes. By huddling together and carefully cupping their hands around their cigarettes, they just managed to keep them alight.

The track ran parallel to what was normally a small burn, but now the storm had transformed it into a roaring, coffee-coloured torrent which raced alongside them, slowing at intervals in ominous, foam-flecked whirlpools, then plunging on down through the glen. A dead sheep went tumbling past in the rushing water, stiff legs pirouetting madly. The Beaters watched as it was swept away downstream.

"Poor basturd, it'll be gettin' hell o' a dizzy!"

They arrived at a sharp dip in the track where the vehicles normally slowed to a crawl - but this time Grallocher jammed his foot hard on the accelerator.

"Whit's the mad basturd doin' now?" cried one of the Beaters anxiously, as the trailer bounced and jolted with ever-increasing speed down the steep incline. What they could not see, but which had filled Grallocher's black heart with sudden joy, was the deep pool of flood water at the bottom of the slope. Like a lifeboat leaving the slipway into the teeth of a Force 10, the Land Rover and trailer disappeared for several seconds in a stupendous cloud of spray. The Beaters emerged, stunned, speechless, paralysed with shock and, as they started up the next hill, the foot's depth of water in the trailer rushed to the back like a miniature tidal wave, almost washing several of them overboard. Every single cigarette was extinguished. An oxy-acetylene blowtorch would not have re-kindled the drooping wads of soggy paper and waterlogged tobacco which the Beaters still held pinched between dripping fingers.

Grallocher glanced in his rear-view mirror. Above the roar of the engine he could hear nothing, but he could see the drenched figures, the waving fists, and the mouths soundlessly screaming abuse. He settled down in his seat and concentrated on the road ahead.

"Aye" he thought, "it's no' been a bad day so far."

In the distance the Major's whistle shrilled.
"OK, boys" said Willie, "let's be havin' you."
The Beaters shuffled together then, on the command, they scampered towards the top of the hill. When they burst on to the open ground they were still in a solid huddle, but with the fierce buffeting of the wind and hampered by the squelching bog underfoot they soon became strung out, the fittest making good progress while their slower companions stumbled along with an ever-increasing sense of panic as they lagged behind. They were only vaguely aware of the distant banging of the guns, their minds concentrating on getting across the strip of open ground as fast as possible.

The procession of Beaters, flapping and jerking in slow motion along the sky-line, should have presented an easy target for the shooters, but the gusting wind made accuracy impossible and, to the Guests' disappointment, every Beater appeared to escape unscathed.

They straggled into the sheltered hollow in the lee of the hill, and stretched out, exhausted, in their tattered oilskins. Grallocher would appear at any moment but, for the minute, just to be sheltered from the battering wind was exquisite pleasure. They lay on their backs and watched the low clouds scudding overhead. It was peaceful, so peaceful. Suddenly, one of them jerked upright, head tilted at an angle, listening. Several others sat up ... they stared at each other, uncomprehending ... carried intermittently on the wind they could hear ... voices! Snatches of song!

"I love to go .. wandering .. mountain track .."

Every Beater was alert now: they could all hear it. On hands and knees they scrambled to the edge of the hollow and peered over.

"Val de ree, val de ra, val de ree, val da ha-ha-ha-ha ... "

The Beaters stared at each other, slack-jawed with astonishment, then their faces cracked into broad grins.

"Let's do the basturds!"

The party of hill walkers aged visibly in the next few seconds. They had been tramping along, breathing in great draughts of fresh air, admiring the scenery, soaking up the ambience when, suddenly, a rabble of screaming scarecrows appeared from nowhere and fell upon them.

"Geez that raincoat, ya big streak o' shite."

The team leader was a tall, fresh-faced, strapping chap, and he had to bend down to reply to the diminutive Beater.

"It's not a raincoat, sonny, it's a cagoule."

No-one saw the small Beater move, but suddenly the hill walker was rolling in the heather, both hands clutching his groin, eyes bulging like a constipated frog.

"C'mon, ya wee basturd" remonstrated Willie, "ye didnae huv tae hit the boy!"

"Honest, Willie, ah never laid a hand oan 'im!"

This was true. No hands were involved - but a lightning head-butt to the crotch can be very painful.

The small Beater puffed out his chest and struck a pose in his newly-acquired rainwear, which reached almost to his ankles.

"Christ, wait till the wimmen see ma new ... CAGOULE ... ah'll huv tae beat them aff wi' a stick!"

There was no further resistance from the hill walkers who huddled in a disconsolate knot as the Beaters proceeded to ransack their equipment. Like a pack of terriers in a rabbit warren they burrowed deep into the bulging rucksacks, bottoms in the air, heads out of sight. As though each rucksack had exploded, their contents soon lay in a radius around them; maps, compasses, water-bottles, bandages, flash-lights, scattered on the ground. From inside one came a muffled cry of triumph, and a Beater emerged holding aloft a Mars bar. This spurred his fellows on to greater efforts and soon they were haggling noisily over chocolate, glucose sweets and assorted fruit and biscuits. One Beater held a small, triangular sandwich between finger and thumb and inspected it closely.

"Check this out, boys" he said in tones of disgust, "it's no' even got a crust on it!"

One of the hill walkers stiffened and stared up the hill.

"Oh God, no!" he gasped, "there's more of them!"

But it was only Grallocher, roaring and screaming at his errant charges. The Beaters straggled back up the hill, impervious to his ranting abuse, passing favourable comments on each other's newly-acquired outdoor wear.

"Aye, that colour really suits you. Goes wi' yer eyes."

"Feel this material. Jist the best!"

"Whit dae ye think o' the cut o' this anorak? Smart, eh!"

"Aye, an' that's a handy poacket fur yer crampons."

"No use tae me, ah huvnae started ma periods yet."

At the bottom of the hill, the walkers glumly picked over the assortment of tattered oilskins and patched raincoats abandoned by their assailants. They wore that expression of mingled distaste and disappointment often seen on the faces of women who have arrived late for a jumble sale and missed the bargains.

On their second charge across the hill the Beaters exceeded all previous speed records. They had the wind behind them this time, and they were running down a slight incline, but what really spurred them on was the fear of getting holes shot in their new outfits. On this occasion Fate smiled upon them, and they came through unscathed.

Afterwards, as they bounced along the track heading back to the Lodge, they sang happily:

"Val de ree, val de ra, val de ree, val da ha-ha-ha-ha ..."

Grallocher's knuckles were white as he gripped the steering wheel, but a strange smile flitted across his dark features - the water-filled dip in the road was just ahead! As the Land Rover slowly crested the hill he hunched down behind the wheel, then jammed the accelerator hard against the floor.

With the trailer bucking and clattering behind, the Land Rover roared down the slope and vanished in a massive cloud of spray at the bottom. As it ground its way out of the flood-water Grallocher turned and squinted expectantly through the rivulets streaming down the back window. He stared, and stared. The little buggers, they were nowhere to be seen. Christ! What had happened? Then he saw the crocodile of Beaters skipping down the hill.

"Val de ree, val de ra ... "

A vein throbbed purply in Grallocher's temple. The cunning little shits, they had gone and baled out at the top of the hill.

The Beaters clambered into the trailer, wreathed in smiles. Some of them waved cheerily to Grallocher.

"Aye" he thought, "it's been a real basturd o' a day!"

CHAPTER 11

Inverdruel basked in the crisp autumn sunshine. The early-morning mist had burned away and the grass in the village square was covered with a sparkling carpet of dew diamonds.

A huddle of pensioners clustered outside the Post Office, discussing the latest outbreak of fornication while they waited for the Saturday papers to arrive. The result of a previous outbreak burped contentedly in its pram parked beside the weighing machine, the needle of which was jammed at eighteen-and-a-half stones. It had been this way ever since one of the local Weightwatchers had attempted to check her progress - visible and enduring testimony to her spectacular lack of success.

The Oldest Inhabitant stood in her doorway and sucked on her pipe, occasionally grinning vacuously at nothing in particular. Neither she nor the few other people gathered in the square noticed the bright pinpoints of light flashing in the distance, where the road came snaking down through the hills. Nor did they pay any attention at first to the faint drone which died away, grew louder, then faded again.

Suddenly it was close, very close, an ever-increasing rumble which grew and grew, until the ground itself seemed to tremble. The Oldest Inhabitant's gums tightened on her pipe-stem, and the infant's dimpled knuckles whitened as it gripped the edge of its pram and peered out fearfully. The pensioners' discussion faltered, just at the point of orgasm - and the weighing machine gave a loud PING and shot back to register zero.

From nowhere a cloud appeared in the clear sky, obscuring the sun and casting a sudden chill. The narrow street began to throb with a roaring, pulsating growl which reverberated and echoed from the stone walls. Curtains twitched, keys rasped in locks, normally savage dogs skulked away down side streets, as the line of Bikers slowly advanced, two abreast, and riding at the head of the column, the personification of evil himself, the dreaded ... Billy Grunter.

He hunched astride a huge black motorcycle, his enormous stomach resting on the petrol tank and quivering in tune with the engine's vibration. His monstrous head slowly swivelled and rays of cold malice flashed from the fishy eyes behind the wire-framed spectacles. Mounted on the front of his bike, tusks curved menacingly, dark eye sockets staring, was the bleached skull of a wild boar. On the back of Grunter's sleeveless denim jacket was the emblem of a boar's head, tusks dripping with blood and below, in black Gothic letters, the legend: "The Dark Avenging Angels."

Yes, it was the most feared bikers' outfit in the North - and they had come to Inverdruel for the weekend.

The rumbling procession of motorcycles growled to a halt outside the hotel. Grunter slowly looked around the deserted square then, leaning ponderously to one side, he spat: a great mucous gobbet, which plopped heavily into the dust at the edge of the pavement. A dribble of saliva left a thin trail across the toe of his boot. Grunter stared stonily into the middle distance, fat fingers thrumming impatiently on the handlebars of his bike. His cohorts glanced nervously at one another, then one, more perceptive than his fellows, scrambled off his motorcycle, prostrated himself at Grunter's feet, and industriously wiped the boot clean with the sleeve of his shirt.

Still staring ahead expressionlessly, Grunter snapped his fingers, and two of his lieutenants scuttled up. One gripped the handlebars tightly, the other braced himself as Grunter leant heavily on him and struggled to swing his massive leg across the bike.

"Ow, ow, YARROO!" he roared, as his leg stuck, then suddenly swung free.

This was the dreaded Billy Grunter, whose name had become a byword for cruelty and destruction, whose marauding gang of Bikers left a trail of broken bones, smashed glass and unplanned pregnancies across the length and breadth of the land. The same Billy Grunter who demanded protection money from Eventide Homes, who ran down lollipop ladies at school crossings, who once tied a traffic warden behind his bike and dragged him, screaming, the wrong way up a one-way street then, in a final act of senseless cruelty, left his groaning, friction-burned victim on double yellow lines.

In corners at Hell's Angels' conventions it was whispered that Grunter had once attended boarding school in England. According to the rumours, he had been the subject of constant bullying and had become disillusioned with academia. Apparently, one fateful day, he overloaded on a particularly powerful sherry trifle, and thus were sown the seeds of his descent into the abyss of alcoholism and violence.

Now, as leader of The Dark Avenging Angels, he was exacting a terrible retribution on a world which had once reviled him, beaten him, and stolen his buns.

Followed at a respectful distance by his ferocious-looking troops, he waddled stiffly towards the door of the public bar.

CHAPTER 12

It had been a tiring week, squelching desperately across the boggy hill under the constant lash of Grallocher's tongue, but now the Beaters were scrubbed and primped and they swayed contentedly to the soporific motion of the bus. Up ahead, the lights of downtown Inverdruel twinkled invitingly in the gathering dusk.

Displaying a sinuosity normally associated with the Paris catwalk, a small Beater sashayed down the gangway, lost inside the folds of his brightly coloured cagoule. Ignoring the rising crescendo of wolf whistles which followed his progress, he confidently outlined the devastating effect he was about to have on the women of Inverdruel.

Suddenly, in mid-sashay, he froze, gaping out of the window ...

" ...wid ye look at THAT!"

Grallocher wrestled with the wheel, cursing violently, as the bus slewed, thrown off balance by the headlong stampede of Beaters to one side of the vehicle. Wide-eyed, they stared at the row of gleaming motorcycles and the circle of tents pitched in a grassy hollow beside them. They stared at the tent, larger than the rest, which was pitched in the middle of the circle. There was a pole beside it, and stuck on top of the pole ... a skull! It was a horrible skull, a long snout with two curved tusks and black eye sockets which, in the half light, seemed to follow them as they drove past.

" ... bloody hell!"

The Beaters glanced nervously at one another as the bus rumbled on into the village.

The streets were unusually quiet as they rolled to a stop outside the hotel. Apprehensively, they descended from the bus and made their way cautiously towards the bar. As they entered, those in front stopped inside the door but those at the back continued pushing forward, creating a log-jam of bodies ...

The whole bar was full of Dark Avenging Angels. They were everywhere, tattooed, leather-jacketed, bearded, metal-studded, practising menacing looks on one another. Instinctively, the Beaters bunched together in their defensive formation, and crabbed sideways towards the bar, hoping not to arouse the attentions of the milling Neanderthals. In muted tones they placed their orders, at the same time nervously taking stock of the situation around them.

"Psssst, boys! Catch an eyeful o' that!"

They glanced surreptitiously in the direction the Beater was indicating with twitching motions of his head.

"Fuck me! What is it?"

"Ah don't know, but it's a big one!"

"Take a gander at the fizzog - looks like a burst arse!"

"Ssh, no' so loud, boys, no' so loud!"

In the alcove, roasting his massive bulk by the log fire, sat Billy Grunter. He squatted like a great, blubbery Buddha, surrounded on either side by attentive acolytes. Another crouched before him, holding up a large plateful of chips. At intervals Grunter reached absent-mindedly towards them with groping, sausage-like fingers. His pink jowls were shiny with grease and they wobbled and quivered as he gorged on the chips, fistfuls at a time. There was a muffled roar, and the fire flared briefly as he leaned to one side and gave vent to a rumble of flatulence. Pushing away the plate, he snapped his fingers peevishly and a henchman scuttled over from the bar bearing a foaming tankard of ale.

At that moment the rear door burst open and the Inverdruel Rockettes marched in, smiling broadly, and none more broadly than Flintstone, who was still enjoying the novelty of his new set of dentures. He flashed dazzling smiles to right and left, the smile slowly becoming fixed as it dawned upon him that something was wrong. Very, very wrong.

"Whit ur you grinnin' at, shit-face?"

Flintstone's sphincter tied itself into a double reef knot.

"Ah, ah ... ah'm no grinnin'" he stammered, his smile growing involuntarily wider as he felt the clammy hand of fear grip his insides, and twist.

"God!" he thought, "must be the wrong pub."

But no, from the corner of his eye he saw the Beaters huddled at the bar, and Andromeda looking over anxiously.

The large, hairy Biker spoke again, in tones dripping with menace.

"You arseholes play Heavy Metal?"

"Em, sure, aye, all the time ... "

The other members of the Rockettes nodded their heads vigorously.

"Heavy Metal. Love it. Play it all the time."

"OK" growled the Biker, "an' fur the last time, get rid o' that stupit smile or ye'll be tastin' ma knuckles."

There was a gentle 'plop' as Flintstone plucked out his dentures and tucked the offending smile out of sight in his shirt pocket.

There was no chance of the Beaters trying out any new dance steps that night. Every female who could be described as even remotely nubile - and most of the Inverdruel females could only be described as remotely nubile - had been locked away by anxious parents. Besides, there was no room to dance. The end of the bar was a seething mass of hair, denim and studded leather as the Bikers, like drought-crazed bison round a dried-up waterhole, shuffled and grunted dementedly to the pulverising beat of Flintstone's guitar.

They had threatened the Rockettes with a slow, horrible death if they failed to produce maximum volume, and the strain was beginning to tell. Flintstone's guitar gave off an acrid smell of burning plastic and, periodically, bright blue sparks rose up from the amplifier like miniature distress flares.

The door opened, and Cynthia slipped in, accompanied by Henri Piptraud and Dolly. They flinched under the ear-blistering decibelic onslaught and stared in amazement at the far end of the bar, where the bearded berserks pounded the floorboards in a maelstrom of stomping feet and pumping elbows.

A loud bellow rumbled over from the direction of the alcove. Grunter was petulantly snapping his fingers, his great moon face quivering with impatience. Several Bikers rushed to his side and, one heaving on either arm and another pushing from behind, they manoeuvred him onto his feet. He stretched, and let loose a deep, reverberating fart, then, like some gross, leering cherub, he lumbered ponderously across the room, his henchmen clearing people from his path as though they were peasants before royalty. Cynthia turned and gave a startled squeal as Grunter loomed over her. She shrank back as his arms reached out and his little rose-bud lips puckered ... ... there was a swish, and a loud crack. The expression on Grunter's face slowly changed from one of porcine lust to one of puzzled incomprehension. Then his eyes rolled upwards, his legs wobbled and, with a mighty WHUMMPF which rattled every glass in the bar, he crashed to the floor.

CHAPTER 13

"Wuz that, or wuz that no', fuckin' SCARY?"

"Yer no' jokin'! That Grunter - ye ever see anythin' like it? Whit a moanster!"

"Willie took a fair skelp oan the turnip. He'll huv a nasty lump the morn."

"He'll huv a nasty lump aw right - an' it'll no' be on his napper. Ah think he's up there jist noo doin' the Romeo 'n' Julius business wi' Cynthia."

"Ye've no proof. It's mebbe wan o' they plutonic relationships, ye know, a wee snog an' that, but she keeps her drawers oan."

"Plutonic, my arse!"

"It's OK fur youse" grumbled the smallest Beater, "look at ma fuckin' cagoule! Wan o' the sleeves is still in Inverdruel."

"Hud yer wheesht, wee man. Yer bloody lucky yer arm's no' still inside it. Speakin' o' which, if big Andromeda jalouses that Willie's hobnobbin' wi' Cynthia -she'll pull mair'n his arm oaf!"

"Gawd, aye! She'll roast his bits o'er a candle."

A shudder ran through the company as they contemplated the marrow-melting prospect of Andromeda's wrath ...

When Willie had pool-cued Grunter in the bar, the Beaters' reactions had been instinctive - blind panic. A brief but ferocious melee had ensued as they became wedged in the doorway and were set upon by the Bikers, who were stunned at the magnitude of the outrage perpetrated on their leader. Fighting a desperate rearguard action, the Beaters scrambled onto the bus and, with Grallocher gunning the accelerator as if his life depended upon it - which it probably did - they rattled out of Inverdruel under a hail of beer cans, stones and death-threats.

One of the Beaters looked round anxiously.

"Where's Willie?"

They stared at each other.

" We've left him behind! Stop the bus, Grallocher!"

"Ah seen him gettin' a dunt on the napper. Wan o' they biker basturds clocked him wi' a bottle."

"Whoa! Stop the bus!"

Suddenly, headlights filled the rear window and the estate Land Rover roared alongside, tooting its horn. Willie's swollen face grinned up at them from the passenger window. He gave a metronomic wave, as practised by Her Majesty when driving past the lower orders.

"The jammy basturd! He's travellin' in style. Wi' Cynthia!"

By the time the Beaters got back the Land Rover was already parked in front of the Lodge. They clattered into the Bothy, but there was no sign of Willie ...

"Anyway, boys, let's get doon tae the business in hand. We canny let those hairy basturds off wi' this. Ah mean, we scarpered like a bunch o' clarty-arsed weans. AND we left Willie behind 'n' aw."

"Aye, we've got wur reputations tae think aboot. We'll huv tae get revenge."

"They're awfy big basturds, though. An' there's lots o' them."

"Are you scairt or somethin'?"

"Naw - ah'd jist like to be there tae blaw oot the candles oan ma next burthday."

"Well, youse lot can please yersels - ah'm gonny find the rotten shite that tore the sleeve aff ma cagoule - an' ah'm gonny gubb the basturd. An' ah doan' care how big he is or how hairy he is or how many pals he's got - ah'm gonny gubb 'im."

"That's the spirit, wee man!"

"The element o' surprise", a Beater said, thoughtfully.

"Whit ur you jibberin' aboot - 'the element o' surprise'?"

"Well, we could nab the basturds while they're asleep, couldn't we? Steam in an' kick the livin' crap oot o' them afore they've a chance tae unbutton their nighties."

"Aye, smart thinkin'. But it'll take mair'n an oor tae hoof aw the way back there, an' it's the middle o' the night, an' it's as black as a miner's arsehole."

"Whut if we grab a few 'oors kip, an' leave furst thing - aboot five o'clock, say - long afore they'll be oot o' their scratchers, an' we get right in there an' blooter them."

"Aye, brilliant, but we'll huv tae work it oot proper ... "

In a mood of rising excitement the Beaters crowded round the table and began to plan their revenge attack. The unshaded glare from the single bulb dangling at the end of the Bothy gave their faces an exaggerated animation, making them appear even more hideous than usual. Its low light threw huge shadows on the far wall - a huddle of dark giants, mimicking every movement of the animated goblins plotting below.

The sudden shriek of the alarm pierced the darkness, drilling remorselessly into the muggy subconscious of the slumbering Beaters, despoiling dreams and giving nightmares noisy substance. A wild swipe connected and sent the clock clattering into a corner, where it continued to trill furiously. Beaters levered themselves from their beds, cursing and swearing and colliding violently in the darkness. A lucky kick sent the clock spinning against the wall. It was still ringing, but quietly now. It was mortally injured.

The light snapped on and the Beaters squinted under its blinding glare, tousled, crumpled and disorientated.

"Aw, c'moan guys" leave's alone."

"Pit that fuckin' light oot!"

But there was no mercy for the laggards. Those beds which still contained inert mounds were pummelled and battered until their defenders' resistance was broken and they crawled, grumbling, from under the blankets.

A kettle bubbled on the stove. One of the Beaters poured a jar of instant coffee into a pan and topped it up with boiling water.

"Coffee, boys" he shouted, a wild exaggeration.

"Mair like bloody sump oil!" muttered a Beater, picking lumps of undissolved coffee powder from between his teeth with a blackened nail. The invigorating brew hit their stomachs with the force of an electric shock. Like a flame along a trail of petrol, it roared through their nervous systems, jump-starting torpid brain cells and burning away the last vestigial remnants of sleep with blowtorch intensity.

"By Christ, that was a good cup o' coffee" said the Beater who had made it, smacking his lips. After several seconds, the total silence registered with him. He looked up and gave a sudden start, as a dozen pairs of eyes glared at him, bright with menace.

"Well, boys, let's do it."

"Aye ... let's stiffen the basturds."

Galvanised now at the prospect of action, they scuttled about, hauling on jackets and woolly bonnets, and sorting out the pile of weaponry assembled the previous evening: an awe-inspiring collection of clubs, bits of fence-post, garden tools, broom handles, stone-filled socks. One Beater took practice swings with a rusty toilet chain.

"OK, lads, let's kick butt!"

The Bothy door crashed open and they poured out into the all-enveloping night.

A dull yellow moon peeped suspiciously through the trees as they marched down the drive, passed between the Major's balls and out onto the main track. The silvered ribbon of road snaked between the dark, looming mounds of the surrounding hills and like a large spiky insect the cluster of heavily-armed Beaters scuttled nervously along. As the road twisted and turned, then dipped suddenly into the dark bowl of the glen, they pressed closer together. They were basically city boys, and they preferred their darkness well peppered with neon. The ill-defined shadows, the small unseen scufflings in the undergrowth, the cold sibilant whisper of the night breeze, the sudden groan of a broken pine bough as they passed beneath it, the evil gurgle of a burn echoing through a culvert, all gradually conspired to send a cold chill seeping into their hearts. As they rounded a bend in a tight huddle, the small Beater in front suddenly stopped dead in his tracks.

"Oh, mammy" he groaned in a strangled whisper, "there's somethin' there ... "

The Beaters pressed nervously together, ears cocked to catch the slightest sound, eyeballs straining to penetrate the claustrophobic gloom which enveloped them.

"What is it?" they whispered.

"There's nothin' there ... "

The moon edged out from behind a low bank of cloud.

"Aaaaaarrrghk!" screamed the small Beater.

Barring their path, a dark silhouette loomed suddenly before them on the crest of the hill. Then it was joined, as if from nowhere, by other black, silent forms.

" ... they've got horns!" wailed the small Beater, turning his head away and squeezing his eyes tightly shut. He thrust his arms out before him, forefingers crossed - it worked for Peter Cushing.

The horned demons turned and clattered off down the road, their woolly rumps quivering with indignation.

"You stupid little fucker ..." BIFF "It's only" ... SMACK ... "a herd o'" ... THUMP ... "bloody" ... THUMP ... "sheep!" THUMP.

Perhaps the unfortunate Beater deserved a spot of chastisement but, at the same time, his companions were grateful for the cover it provided for their own embarrassment. They had all experienced a few seconds of gut-wrenching terror, and several bladders had teetered on the brink of disaster.

Once more they set off, the small Beater trailing behind, rubbing his bruised body and muttering unhappily. When they finally climbed out of the dark glen, a dirty smudge of light had begun to streak the sky over the low hills to the east. The fervour with which they had set out was now replaced by a growing tension and unease, and they shivered in the cold, dank air. The darkness had been cover of a sort but, as the sky rapidly lightened, they felt small and exposed and they suddenly became very conscious that every footstep was taking them closer to ... Grunter.

The Beaters crouched along the edge of the low ridge and stared down at Grunter's encampment. Wraiths of clammy early-morning mist swirled slowly in the hollow, giving the circle of tents a frozen, ghostly appearance. Beyond them, like a row of tethered animals, the bikes were parked. From the tents, dulled by the damp, heavy air, and set against a background drone of snoring, came the sound of muted intestinal rumbling, punctuated at intervals by long, gentle, puttering farts. It was a scene of almost Biblical charm. Then a thin shroud of mist drifted away, to reveal the sinister skull perched on top of its pole.

"Oh, mammy", whispered the smallest Beater.

There could be no going back now. Hearts hammering in their chests, legs shaking, knuckles white as they gripped their makeshift weapons, the Beaters crept down the slope, picking their way carefully in the wet grass. Communicating in barely audible whispers and extravagant sign-language, they fanned out and slipped silently between the tents. They took up position and nodded to one another,

"GET ... THE ... BASTURDS!"

A cacophony of howls, oaths and groans echoed around the hollow as the Beaters kicked and bludgeoned the lumps which appeared and disappeared under the thrashing canvas. Trapped inside their tents, befuddled, and cocooned in sleeping bags, the Bikers stood no chance. Those who managed to scramble out were immediately set upon by an angry swarm of Beaters who made up for their lack of stature with a virtuoso display of the martial arts. The Flyin' Heid Butt, the Poke in the Eye, and the Swift Boot to the Balls featured strongly, either performed as individual works of art or in aesthetically pleasing combinations.

The most violent assault was on Grunter's tent. The Beaters prodded and thwacked at the heaving mound of canvas, provoking screams of outrage and pain.

"Ow! Ow! Gerroff! Yarroo!"

When the Beaters finally scampered from the field of battle, they triumphantly bore aloft the boar's skull on the end of the pole. They stopped at the top of the hill and turned to survey the battleground. A chorus of obscenities drifted up from the battered Bikers, but they made no attempt to follow them. The Beaters grinned at each other, then set off on the road back to Glendruel.

"See this pig's heid" suggested one, "let's call it 'Grallocher'!"

It was mid-morning when Willie strode into the Bothy. His tuneless whistling and air of desperate nonchalance provided no cover at all for his manifest embarrassment. Not one of the Beaters looked up. It was not so much a silence, more a complete and total lack of any sound whatsoever. A fly's fart would have produced an echo.

"Wunner where Willie went last night?"

"Dunno. His bed's no' been slept in."

"Mebbe he's got ambrosia. He did take a fair dunt oan the napper frae that bottle."

"Aye, that'll be it. He'll huv been wannerin' aboot the grounds wi' his mind jist a blank."

"Fuck me! That could be dodgy. The Beast might have spotted him!"

"Shut it, you basturds" warned Willie. "Youse cannae speak. Whit huv youse been up tae anyway? Ah leave you fur a coupla' oors an' next thing there's a fuckin' pig's heid oan the table!"

"A little prezzie for you Willie. From the Bikers. But, no tae change the subject. Tell us, Willie - wur ye flingin' yer puddin'?"

"You boys are totally disgustin'. Ah'm off tae see Cook fur a spot o' grub."

And, with more speed than dignity, he hurried from the Bothy.

The Beaters looked at each other, eyebrows arched in mock horror.

"Disgustin', is it? DISGUSTIN! Well, ah never! Young people nowadays!"

"Aye, at least we jist have wan burd oan the string at a time. He's knockin' off two wimmen. That's bigotry. Ye can get the jile fur that!"

"Aye, we live in terrible times, so we do."

"An' he never even said 'thank you' for that lovely skull."

"Och, the boy's in love. His heid's in the clouds."

"But whit does a classy wee burd like Cynthia see in that big ugly brute? Ah mean, why'd she want an animal like Willie trampin' aboot in her androgenous zones?"

"Well, he did save her from Grunter's clutches. Ah mean tae say, Grunter wiz fixed up tae do aw kinds o' unspeakable things to her an' then toss aside her bruised an' bleedin' body like an old rag doll, wance he'd satisfied his evil animal lusts. An' Willie pops up an' saves her from aw that. Wimmen do appreciate these thoughtful little gestures, ye know!"

"Aye, ah suppose. But whit ah'd like tae know is, who's gonny pop up an' save Willie when big Andromeda tosses aside HIS bruised an' bleedin' body?"

"Aye ... there's a thing."

CHAPTER 14

Ploppwaft and Grobbelwoenck were driven down to Inverdruel Station first thing in the morning to catch the early train. Blatch's departure was a less subdued affair. The crescendo of horn-tooting brought the Beaters pouring from the Bothy to see what was happening. They were just in time to see Blatch's round, jolly face beaming from behind the wheel of the vintage roadster as it described an extravagant turn in front of the House, then roared off down the drive in a spray of gravel.

Tarquin Ross-Pettle watched it go. He half raised his arm and opened his mouth, as if to say something, but no sound came. Then his shoulders drooped and, staring, dull-eyed at the crumpled cheque in his hand, he turned and walked slowly back to the House.

"Bah, y'awl!"

The Beaters stared as Dolly's farewell trill pierced their eardrums. The Land Rover rumbled past, Grallocher at the wheel, Piptraud squeezed happily in the middle. Dolly hung from the window, podgy arm waving enthusiastically.

"Aw rev-wire y'awl!"

There was a tinkle, as the stone from her engagement ring bounced on the gravel. Then they were gone.

Sunday lunch was always a high-spirited occasion. The Beaters usually had a proportion of the previous night's alcohol sloshing along their arteries and any love-bites on their necks had not had time to fade. Love-bites were the only generally-accepted proof that a bull's-eye had been scored on the dartboard of love. Some of the uglier Beaters were occasionally accused of inflicting love-bites on themselves in order to achieve status. One particularly unappealing Beater had appeared on several consecutive Sundays with a mass of purple bruises on his neck. This caused incredulity, and also a certain amount of jealousy, to stir in the breasts of his unmarked comrades. All enquiries were met by a grotesque pantomime of smirking, winking and nose-tapping. Then one Sunday morning the unlikely Adonis overslept, only to be woken by the hysterical screams of his associates, who had spotted the bulldog clips he had attached to his neck the previous evening.

On this particular Sunday the Beaters were feeling exceptionally jolly because, quite apart from their trouncing of the Bikers, it was also the smallest Beater's birthday. Cook had, of course, pulled out all the stops. They had just finished large helpings of 'Biff à la Mode' (with Turnip Macedoine) and, instead of the usual Sunday treat of Spotted Dick, Cook had made Jelly.

At the scrapyard where she had purchased her cauldron she had haggled so fiercely with the proprietor that he had had to throw in a job lot of a dozen aluminium jelly-moulds just to clinch a break-even deal. Cook saved them for special occasions.

The Birthday Boy sat in the place of honour at the end of the table, peering out from under a paper party hat. It was only his prominent ears that prevented it from becoming a cummerbund. He was half concealed behind a large, translucent green rabbit. Up and down either side of the table other rabbits, green, red, yellow and orange, quivered and wobbled alarmingly. The Birthday Boy had a whole rabbit all to himself, but the others had to share one between two. Bartering began immediately:

"Who's wantin' orange lugs?"

"Ah'll take wan orange lug aff ye for wan red paw."

"Ah've a green nose here. Any takers fur a nice green nose?"

Ah'll swap a bit o' ma orange heid fur a bit o' yer yella arse."

"No way - this yella arse is lovely."

After the jelly came the highlight. The Cake! Cook's biceps strained as she steered it across the room, banked steeply and brought it in to land in front of the smallest Beater. It was a massive chocolate job, studded with candles. Cook whipped out a box of matches and lit up. There was a brief babble of noise while bets were hurriedly placed on how many candles would be snuffed out with one blow; then an expectant silence. The smallest Beater rose to his feet and eyed up The Cake. Then he started to inflate ...

A lot of the smart money was against him because he had been a heavy smoker since the age of four: however, though they creaked and whistled a bit as they approached maximum capacity, his lungs had the tensile strength of a cowboy's underpants. The punters had also reckoned without the fact that he had no front teeth and, when he finally exhaled, the blast of air and saliva which roared through the gap not only extinguished all the candles but also threatened to lift the slab of icing off the top of the cake ...

When the hubbub had died down, Cook approached and handed the Birthday Boy a parcel.

"Aw, Cook, ye shouldn't huv" he said, eagerly ripping off the paper.

"Ma cagoule!"

Cook had sewn on a new sleeve. The only material to hand had been stiff canvas and when the Beater tried it on the sleeve tended to project from his body, but he was obviously delighted and refused to take it off even to eat his cake, though it meant holding the chocolate wedge at arm's length and swinging his whole body round to take a bite.

That night, Willie and Cynthia wandered slowly down the winding path which led through the rhododendrons to the edge of the stream. Far above them, like a scatter of diamond dust against the blue-black velvet of the sky, a myriad light-points shimmered and sparkled. A swift-moving Perseid glowed briefly among the stars, fading as silently and suddenly as it had appeared. Willie and Cynthia walked side by side, not touching and hardly speaking, but the electricity of love whispered and crackled gently all around them. Cynthia's privileged and protected upbringing had insulated her from much of life's unpleasantness - and Willie's uncouthness, his bedraggled appearance, his inadequate contact with soap and water, were all too real - but these things had ceased to be of any importance. The hand of Fate had drawn two pieces from the giant jigsaw box of life; two pieces which, against all the odds, fitted perfectly together.

In the far darkness the scream of a rabbit was cut short as a passing fox bit its head off. Cynthia shivered and moved closer to Willie, her cheek soft against the rough material of his jersey. She gave a slight gasp as she felt the hard lump pressing against her inner thigh.

"Sorry about that" said Willie, and transferred his Swiss Army knife to his back pocket.

CHAPTER 15

A Beater scrunched across the gravel in front of the Lodge as Stratford Hathaway assisted his wife, Lavinia, and her French poodle, Fluffles, from the large Mercedes. Unintentionally, the Beater let fly with a brief squirt of wind - the Turnip Macedoine serving notice that it was about to enter the final straight after completing several laps of his lower intestine. Stratford clasped one hand to his heart, flung the other heavenwards, and declaimed in ringing tones, which boomed and echoed around the forecourt:

"Hail, gentle zephyr, on thy balmy breath sweet Autumn's scent transported!"

The Beater looked startled and quickened his pace, glancing back nervously over his shoulder as he headed for the sanctuary of the Bothy.

Stratford Hathaway, one of London's top theatrical directors, was taking a well-earned break before starting work on his next production. Clad in cricketing jersey, silk cravat and crumpled corduroy trousers, and with a lock of hair falling elegantly over one eye, he looked like the leading character from one of his own plays.

His wife Lavinia, a vision in tulle, was ... perfect. She had perfect eyes, perfect teeth and perfect cheekbones.

"I say, I wonder if that rough little chap is one of the fellows we'll be potting at?"

Her diction was perfect, too.

"Whence and what art thou, execrable shape?" boomed Stratford, in the direction of the Bothy towards which the Beater was now scuttling furiously.

"You could be right, darling" he said, "the fellow had a definite 'shot-at' look about him."

And, gently clasping Lavinia's perfectly manicured fingers, Stratford escorted her towards the Lodge. Fluffles trotted behind with precise, dainty steps.

The Major emerged from the main door, followed by Grallocher, and came forward to meet the Hathaways.

"Ah, Manley-Buttocks! So pleased, so pleased!" said Stratford, extending a hand.

"My darling wife, Lavinia, and ... 'Fluffles' - he indicated the poodle, which had begun to sniff at Grallocher's leg. Grallocher's lip took on an almost imperceptible curl. He did not regard poodles as dogs. For a start, dogs did not wear pink bows in their hair. Fluffles stared up at him with her small, beady, knowing eyes and immediately began to yelp furiously. A tremor ran down Grallocher's leg. He clenched his fists - for a brief second a wonderful vision had flitted through his mind, his size eleven boot poised in mid-air, having just completed its swing, and ... 'Fluffles' ... in silhouette, growing rapidly smaller as she completed her trajectory ...

"Did the nasty man frighten you then?" said Lavinia in syrupy tones, as she swept the quivering dog into her arms.

"Ah, yes, Major" said Stratford, "meant to mention that. Fluffles is in an, how shall we say? ... 'interesting' condition."

The Major looked puzzled.

"The bitch is on heat" Grallocher muttered gruffly, out of the corner of his mouth.

Lavinia blanched at the coarseness of the man's language.

"Oh, there's no problem there, no problem at all" the Major said reassuringly, "no dogs here nowadays, sad to say, but we still have the old kennels behind the Lodge. I can guarantee that ... 'Fluffles' ... will be completely safe there. And Grallocher here can give her a spot of exercise in the mornings and evenings ..."

"That's anither Guest appeared" said the Beater to an interested circle of associates in the Bothy.

"Whit's he like?"

"Ah, it's a bloke an' 'is wife. Right plonker. He called me a gentle zeffir."

"Whit's a zeffir?"

"Huvnae a clue, but if ah'm a gentle one, ah'd hate tae meet a wild one."

"Whit's his wife like?"

"Ach, she's got wan o' they faces, ye know the kind - ye'd never get tired o' punchin' it. They've a dug an' aw. Wan o' they poodle things, half bald an' big flappy lugs, looks like its hooter's been jammed in a pencil sharpener."

The Beaters had the day off, due to the arrival of the new Guests, in whom they always took a keen professional interest. Those who turned up with their own guns and the appearance of practised marksmen were sometimes slightly unnerved at the cold stares and obvious hostility of any Beaters they came in contact with, as opposed to the effusive welcome they received from the Manley-Buttockses.

"There's some Irish lad turned up this mornin' as well", continued the Beater. "Got a fizzog like a satsuma. He'd take a pint, by the look o' 'im."

"Aye? Could be a case fur extendin' the hand o' friendship. Anybody know any Val Doonican songs?"

Aloysius Flannelly had arrived earlier in the morning. He had a short, stocky, pugnacious build, and the complexion of a wire-brushed beetroot. The small, tight curls in his flaming orange hair seemed to have been knitted directly onto his scalp. There were no flies on Aloysius Flannelly - and if there had been he would have found a way to process and market them.

He had inherited fifteen acres of boggy ground outside the small town of Knockmagooley, Co Kerry, and this had been the unlikely basis of his fortune. In the many public houses of Knockmagooley envious people referred to him bitterly as the 'Gombeen Man'. If he put a finger in all his pies, they said, he would have to use his toes as well.

On taking over his fifteen acres he had immediately put one acre under clover. In the small factory unit which he erected beside it the clover was pressed and dried, and half-a-dozen women were employed to glue on extra leaves. It was then incorporated into key rings, greetings cards, paperweights, etcetera, and shipped out in bulk containers, mostly to America, where there was a large demand for lucky four-leaved clover.

The Knockmagooley Horse and Donkey Retiral Home took up another thirteen acres. Ancient asses and knackered nags were taken in, their owners departing with lightened wallets, but happy in the knowledge that their animals would be well looked after in their final years. Before they left, some of them called in to the Knockmagooley Pet Food factory, which Aloysius had built on the one-acre plot adjacent to the Horse and Donkey Retiral Home. You could bulk-buy tins of dog or cat food at really competitive prices. The muddy, pot-holed track which led from the pet food factory back on to the main road went past Flannelly's Five Star Car Wash. It did good business.

In the afternoon Grallocher appeared from the station with another Guest. Widgery-Sprocket was a retired diplomat, doddering absent-mindedly towards his ninetieth year. His mind had started to go about the time of the Suez crisis, and it had been downhill ever since. As a tight-lipped Grallocher assisted him out of the Land Rover the small knot of Beaters watching the performance looked at one another, and grinned.

The Guest who most impressed the Beaters was heard before he was seen. The Bothy trembled as a low growl came up through the floorboards and rattled the windows.

"Gawd - sounds like Andromeda!" said a Beater. They dashed to the window, then poured from the door in time to see the massive Cherokee jeep grumbling to a halt.

"Christ!" muttered a Beater, "you could mate that with Grallocher's Land Rover and get tractors!"

It had huge, fat tyres, acres of glittering chrome, and bumpers designed to intimidate charging buffalo. The door swung open and Brent Crude stepped out. He was a giant. He grinned at the Beaters and extended a shovel-like hand.

"Crude's the name an' oil's ma game" he rumbled, crunching their puny digits in his massive paw.

"You boys jest call me Brent, ah doan believe'n stannin' on no ceremony."

He reached into the jeep and fetched out a wide-brimmed stetson, which he adjusted carefully on his head, then he reached in again and produced a case of beer.

"C'd you fellers handle a Bud?"

He passed the beer across to the speechless Beaters.

"Be seein' you, boys", and he grinned, tipped the edge of his hat with a forefinger, and strode off towards the Lodge.

Brent Crude, oil executive, was the last Guest to arrive.

CHAPTER 16

The Beaters enjoyed the next few days. The mornings were crisp, but as the sun shouldered its way through the wreaths of mist and rose into the hard, blue, Autumn sky it soon burned off the sugary dustings of frost. The Beaters scampered across the hill with the heat of the sun on their faces and the ground hard underfoot, and they roared and howled more for the pure pleasure of being alive than from fear of the pellets which buzzed around them.

The Guests delighted in the tranquillity of the quiet wilderness. It washed over them, and the accumulated tensions of their normal lives dissolved unnoticed into the crystal air. The novelty of the bumping, bouncing trip into the hills, the unfamiliar tang of peat and heather, the feel of the earth pressed against their bodies, the explosion and kick of the guns, the acrid scent of gunpowder: all sensations so alien to their normal existence that long-atrophied nerves came tingling to life.

Content though the present party of Guests appeared to be, the Major was still troubled. He was only too well aware that other parties had measured the success of their visit entirely on the number of Beaters knocked over. His last meeting with MacBog still rankled - he knew that further concessions from that department were unlikely. As he racked his brains for a solution to this perennial problem he recalled with a shudder how he had once suggested that, for the benefit of the Guests, when a Beater was hit he should "make the most of it." He had not reckoned on the high proportion of undiscovered thespians lurking in the Beaters' ranks. All over the hill they staggered in circles, clutching their throats, rolling their eyes, pirouetting to the ground in a frenzy of jerking limbs. To make it even more ridiculous, some then lay motionless on their backs with their legs stuck perpendicularly in the air. It had been awful. The Major cringed with embarrassment when he remembered how the Guests had finally laid down their guns and begun to applaud ...

No, he would have to think of something else - and the seed of an idea was slowly taking root in the darker recesses of his mind.

Major Manley-Buttocks had never understood the powerful forces which drove his wife. Her natural urges seemed peculiar and rather frightening to him. Admittedly, he himself occasionally fell prey to strange sensations, vague feelings of tension. When this happened he would descend to the gun room in the basement and reverentially slip out his Purdey. He would run his hand along the gleaming barrel, caress the silk-smooth patina of its walnut butt, heft its satisfying weight in his hand. Then, afterwards, he would invariably experience a deep feeling of relaxation and well-being.

His wife's enthusiasms, however, took a far more immediate and demanding form and eventually he became so worn down from constantly having to take evasive action that, in desperation, he enlisted the aid of Doctor McLush. He secured from him a supply of powerful tranquillisers. Whenever Maud showed signs of going into overdrive he would slip a couple of capsules into her tea and, in no time at all, the dreaded gleam in her eye would flicker and fade.

"Yes!" thought the Major, as the idea crackled suddenly through his brain. "Yes! That's it! I'll feed the little buggers tranquillisers!"

Eagerly he reached for the phone.

"McLush? Yes, Manley-Buttocks here. I'd like a, em ... a private consultation. Can't talk on the phone ... personal matter, y'know. Yes? ... splendid! Good man! And ... I'll have a little, er, something for you. Very well - see you shortly."

He replaced the receiver and leaned back in his chair, hands clasped across his stomach, and breathed a long sigh of satisfaction.

From inside the Bothy the Beaters recognised the tortured scream of Doctor McLush's ancient Morris. They scrambled outside and gathered round the vehicle, admiring the way it was parked at an angle with one front wheel mounted on the grass verge. The driver's door swung open, and McLush tumbled out and began to negotiate the tricky patch of gravel between his car and the Lodge.

The Beaters had been looking forward to the Doctor's next visit. One of them had been saving a lump of Cook's special heavy-duty toffee for just this occasion. Quietly, they opened the passenger door. Jim gazed out sadly, ignoring the fleas which were practising their landing techniques on his forehead. The circle of Beaters smiled encouragement at him, and made enticing noises through puckered lips. Jim stared at them, a shadow of suspicion flickering in his mournful eyes. Then he saw the brown sticky lump in the Beater's hand. He looked up again. They were still smiling. At last, he thought, at last, after all these years of abuse, all these years of being laughed at and mocked, finally a small demonstration of affection. Slowly, he hauled his creaking body out of the car, the sudden movement causing several fleas to crash-land badly.

"Give us a paw, Jim!" said the Beater with the toffee.

Jim raised an arthritic leg a couple of inches off the ground.

"Good boy! Good boy! Here's yer toffee", and Jim's jaws clamped round the tacky amber lump of Cook's finest.

The Major too had noted Doctor McLush's arrival. He hurried across the forecourt to meet him, followed by Grallocher bearing a clinking carrier bag.

"Ah, Doctor, good of you to come so promptly. It's a rather, em, delicate matter. You recall those ... tranquillisers ... you prescribed for Maud? Yes, well, it's the Beaters, you see, they're too, er, lively, and I need a large supply of ... em ... tranquillisers ... to relax them."

"Y'need trank ... lizahs t'r'lax Beat'rs?" slurred the Doctor, his ruddy face puckered with incomprehension.

"Grallocher!"

The clinking bag was passed over.

"Shertainly, Mayshor. You wan' trank ... lizahs, you'll get ... trank ... lizahs! Mus' make note. Wher's ma bag? ... JIM!"

Jim's head swung round at the sound of his master's voice. His jaws were pumping slowly up and down - eating toffee was hard work.

"Bring m'bag Jim!"

Obediently, Jim stuck his head into the car.

"M'bag Jim!"

Jim sat beside the car and stared desperately across at his master, his muzzle writhing in a gruesome parody of a smile, toffee dribbling from his seized-up jowls.

"M'BAG, JIM!"

Jim sat rooted to the spot, whining helplessly, his eyes bulging and rolling in a forlorn attempt at communication.

"Nev'r min' Mayshor. Ah'll see t'your ... pr'scription. Sen' Gralloscher down safter ... noon", and he turned and headed unsteadily back to his car.

POFF! POFF! POFF! Jim's tail lashed the ground with an ever-increasing frenzy as his master approached.

"Usheless, shtupid an'mal" muttered the Doctor.

"Shpen' fortune'n bloody dog bishcits! All those yearsh'a trainin'! Waishta time. Bloody waishta time. Manz bes' fren - my arsh!", and he clambered into the car and slammed the door.

Still whining and dribbling toffee, Jim climbed slowly into the passenger seat, and one of the Beaters swung the door closed behind him.

"Poor basturd. We'll get him liquorice allsorts next time."

The Doctor scrabbled in his medical bag, looking for his notebook and muttering over and over to himself "Trank ... lizahs t'r'lax Beat'rs. Trank ... lizahs t'r'lax Beat'rs."

He finally located his notebook and a couple of minutes later found the pencil stub to go with it. He wrote slowly, mouthing the words, "Mayshor Manley Buttocks. Large supply ... Lax'tives ... t'trank ... lize Beat'rs."

Then he snapped his notebook shut and, with a final withering look at his doleful, dribbling companion, slammed the car into the wrong gear and jolted away down the drive.

CHAPTER 17

Cook made porridge in the old traditional way, the oatmeal being left to soak overnight.

"Bastard!" hissed Grallocher, as he thumped his shin against a wooden bench. He clicked on his torch and played the dull beam around the kitchen. Yes, there it was. He tip-toed across to the big black cauldron sitting in the corner, and peered in. It was full of oatmeal soaking in water. Perfect! With some difficulty he extracted the brown paper bag from his pocket. He frowned. Dammit! No-one had told him how much to put in. He played the feeble light from his torch onto the packet. No instructions. He thought he could make out the words 'SENNA EXTRACT", but they were too indistinct to be sure. What the hell, he thought, and emptied the contents into the cauldron. Then he tip-toed back across the kitchen and let himself out, closing the door slowly and quietly behind him. He glanced around. Not a soul to be seen. With a low chuckle he slunk away.

When Grallocher had arrived at Doctor McLush's house in Inverdruel that afternoon, the Doctor's housekeeper had explained that he was "having a nap", but that he had left a package to be collected. By the time Grallocher returned to the Lodge, the Major was waiting for him impatiently.

"Did you get it?" he asked, before Grallocher was half out of the Land Rover.

"Aye, sur, there ye go."

The Major snatched the small parcel from him, and hugged it to his chest.

"Yes! At last! Now we have the little buggers!"

He had outlined the scenario to Grallocher, dwelling lovingly on every detail.

"They'll be zombies, Grallocher, zombies! They'll be wandering about the hill doped to the eyeballs. Not a care in the world. Think of it! They'll be stopping to pick flowers - picture it, Grallocher! MacBog will be shouting 'Not so fast, boys, not so fast!' Oh yes!" he chortled, holding the parcel out at arm's length and regarding it lovingly, "this is the answer!"

Swept along by the Major's enthusiasm, Grallocher almost smiled.

Next morning, the Beaters poured into the kitchen and waited patiently while Cook gave the porridge a final stir and ladled it onto their plates. As usual, they heaped on jam, syrup, treacle, etcetera, and ate until they were fit to burst. Afterwards, they relaxed for a while with huge mugs of hot, sweet tea.

"OK, boys" said Willie, "let's hit the road."

They straggled round to the front of the Lodge, climbed into their trailer and sat watching as the Guests emerged from the main door.

Widgery-Sprocket doddered down the steps, turned sharp left and shuffled off towards the bushes. Grallocher caught up with him and, gripping him by the shoulders, steered him back towards the other Guests.

"That one almost got away Grallocher."

The Beaters chuckled.

Stratford Hathaway emerged, genteelly assisting his wife down the steps.

"Look!" said one of the Beaters. "That lad's got a Barbie Doll!"

Stratford stopped and looked over at the trailer and its bulging cargo of humanoids.

"How beauteous mankind is" he intoned, eyes raised heavenwards. "O brave new world, that has such people in."

"Is he takin' the piss?"

"Prob'ly. He's the basturd that called me a zeffir."

"Who did that?" a Beater cried out suddenly. "That wid melt asbestos!"

A putrefactive odour had suddenly assailed their nostrils. The culprit chose to remain anonymous.

With the Guests finally loaded up, the Land Rover set off, Grallocher and the Beaters bringing up the rear.

PRRRRRPT!

"Gawd all fucking mighty! Who did that?"

The smell was terrible. Everyone stared at his neighbour accusingly. The smallest Beater said nothing. His face was crimson.

"You little basturd!"

Suddenly, the trailer hit a pot-hole.

PRRRFFT! PRRFWHARRRRF!

"Fuck it, ah'm no' feelin' too good!"

PRROOOFFFT!

The Beaters stared around, eyes wide with fear. Some clutched their stomachs and groaned.

The Land Rover finally lurched to a stop on top of the hill. Grallocher climbed out.

"Oh my God!" he cried, stepping back, his hand over his nose. The Beaters slowly hauled themselves out of the trailer, moaning. Every few seconds there was a rumble, and a Beater would double up and give vent to a long, puttering burst of flatulence.

A whistle sounded in the distance.

"Come on, boys" said Willie, himself ashen-faced. "We better go through the motions."

"Christ!" cried a Beater, hunched in agony, "the motion's ur goin' through me!"

They stumbled half-heartedly up the rise, leaving Grallocher bent over the bonnet of the Land Rover. His face was green. In his whole life he had never smelled anything like it.

As they staggered on to the top of the hill, the point of no return suddenly arrived. The Guests, positioned in the shooting-butts, stared, open-mouthed, as a centipede of screaming Beaters snaked down the hill towards them. The air seemed to shimmer in their wake.

"Jumpin' Jeezus!" cried Aloysius, "they're headin' straight for us!"

"Get back! Get back!" roared the Major, leaping to his feet and flapping his arms.

Widgery-Sprocket got to his feet and began to blast shots into the sky.

The rabble of Beaters poured between the butts, the smallest Beater out in front, screaming in a high-pitched voice:

"Ma arse is on fire! Ma arse is on fire!"

"Holy smoke!" muttered Brent Crude, as the Beaters pounded on and vanished into a thicket of whin bushes which lined the gully at the bottom of the hill. "Those guys sure know how to put on a show!"

Lavinia wept quietly, though not enough to spoil her make-up. Stratford gently patted her hand.

Slowly, the wild thrashing in the bushes subsided, and eventually a straggle of pasty-faced Beaters emerged and began to pick their way slowly back up the hill, taking careful steps. The smallest Beater clutched his backside with both hands.

"Ma rostrum" he sobbed, "it's burned red raw."

Grallocher appeared over the brow of the hill. The Major glared at him. Grallocher said nothing, only shrugging his shoulders helplessly. He was almost past caring.

CHAPTER 18

The Beaters had the next day off. It was just as well, because many were still in a weakened state, though the prospect of the trip to the bright lights of Inverdruel that evening was hastening the recovery process.

Cynthia appeared in the Bothy. When this had first occurred, the Beaters had regarded it as an alien intrusion into their territory, but they had gradually adopted Cynthia as their own and now made her welcome.

"Hi, doll! Ye' lookin' fur the big yin?"

"Yes, we're off on a shopping trip."

"A shoppin' trip! My, my! I hope ye realise that the only shops Willie goes intae is bettin' shops."

"Well, we'll see about that."

"Ho, ho ... WILLIE! ... yer missus is here."

Willie appeared from the wash-room, clutching an off-white towel.

"It's OK, Cynth, he's surrenderin'!"

Willie finished drying his face and flung the towel at the Beater's head.

"Ah hope these animals huvnae been annoyin' you."

"Not at all, Willie, they've just been telling me about your gambling problems."

"Doan believe it, doll, ah only bet on winners, an' if you wuz a filly ah'd bet ma life savins'."

Several of the Beaters made retching noises.

"C'mon, Cynth" said Willie, "let me take you away from this squalor."

It was several hours before the Beaters heard the Land Rover return.

"Aye, that'll be Prince Charming back."

"Ur ye sure? Disnae sound like a pumpkin tae me."

"It's a pumpkin wi' a fucked exhaust!"

The Beaters were still chortling when the door opened and Cynthia came in, followed slowly by Willie.

"Well, boys" said Cynthia brightly, "what do you think?"

The Beaters gaped, open-mouthed, at Willie, then at Cynthia, then back to Willie.

"Lookit the strides! They've got parrlell creases doon them!"

"Ah DO like the jersey, there's somethin' aboot a Fair Isle pattern ... !"

"An' the hair! Ah mean, lookit the hair. Ah never knew Vidal Sassoon hud a branch this far north!.

"Aye, boys, but who is it?"

"No idea, never seen 'im before."

"Looks like wan o' they wallies oot o' the Littlewood's Catalogue."

"Right, you basturds" growled Willie, "that's enough!"

"Tisk, tisk, Willie. Language!" admonished Cynthia sweetly.

"Aye, mind yer language, my man, it disnae go wi' yer hair-cut."

"God, ah widnae be surprised if he's wearin' new Y-fronts ... !"

There was a long, embarrassed silence. Finally Cynthia spoke:

"Well, boys" she said, "I'll have to dash - Guests' dinner to prepare", and she stretched up and planted a little kiss on Willie's crimson cheek.

As she pulled the door closed behind her and set off across to the Lodge, dull thuds and muffled screams could be heard from the Bothy.

The Beaters had just started their evening meal when there was a thunderous knocking on the cookhouse door.

"That'll be Andromeda!"

Willie glared at the comic.

The door swung open and Brent Crude entered, stooping low to avoid the lintel. He straightened up and noticed Cook standing by the cauldron. He removed his hat.

"Howdy, ma'am. Brent's the name. Honoured t'make your acquaintance."

Cook smiled and blushed. She was not used to manners.

"Ah jest popped in t'see how the fellers're doin', after their little ... upset ... on the hill."

"Thanks" said Willie, "we're just aboot recovered."

"Gee, Willie" exclaimed Brent, staring, "ah didn't realahz you were sich a snappy dresser."

The Beaters snorted. Willie glared at them.

"That makes two of us" said the smallest Beater. He was wearing his cagoule.

"That sure does smell good" said Brent, looking at the steaming bowls on the table.

"Haul up a seat" said Cook. "There's plenty more here", and she prodded the contents of the cauldron enthusiastically with her ladle.

"Oh, no, ah couldn't, ma'am" protested Brent.

"Come on, Mr Crude" said a Beater, "park yer arse."

They all shuffled along the bench to make a space at the end.

"Gee, thanks boys" said Brent, "ah'm so hungry ah could eat a skunk's butt raw - beggin' pardon, ma'am - it's jest, the food over at the Lodge - it's nice 'n' all, doan git me wrong, but ah tek a lot a' fillin'! Over there, they serve up that fancy-pants French stuff, an ah like ma meat big."

Cook placed a large bowl, filled to the top, in front of him.

"None o' yer French stuff here, Mr Crude", said the Beater who was sitting next to him, "we're huvin' ragoo."

"An' the big lumps urr ... doughballs."

When they were finished, Brent leaned back and patted his stomach.

"Hog-tie ma ass - that was damn good rations, Cook."

He reached into his pocket and produced a card.

"You keep this, ma'am. You ever need a job, you get'n touch, an' ah'll put you on one of ma rigs. Any'a you boys fancy a see-gar?"

"Aye ... em ... thanks, Mr Crude."

"Whoa there! Y'all call me Brent now", and he handed round the cigars. The Beaters lit up and before long were almost invisible in a thick, fragrant smog. Brent leaned back, eyes half closed, and took a long draw on his cigar. The smallest Beater watched closely. He leaned back too, and inhaled deeply. There was a sudden explosion of retching, and he tumbled backwards in a blur of flailing limbs. Still spluttering, and with tears streaming down his face, he clambered back onto the bench, wheezing and whistling.

"Hog-tie ma ass" he gasped, "that's a damn good cigar."

After their meal the Beaters headed back to the Bothy to start the painstaking process of transforming themselves into sex symbols. No medieval alchemist ever came as close to transmuting base metal into gold as the Beaters managed every Saturday night. Oxters were soaped furiously, talcum powder puffed into socks, rusty razors rasped over stubbled cheeks, after-shave dabbed onto depilated pores, corkscrews of curling hair quiffed under layers of fragrant gel.

"Gawd" said Willie, watching the preparations. "Ah could near fancy you masel'."

"Fuck me" cried a Beater, "he's got two wimmen already an' he fancies us as well! He's like wan o' they Arab boys, wi' their harums."

"By the way Willie, how're ye gonny explain the hair-cut 'n' the new gear tae Andromeda?"

"Ah! Ah wis goin' tae mention that, boys. Ah'm plannin' a ... em ... a quiet night at home."

"A quiet night at home! My arse! Yer gonny be snoggin' wi' Cynthia an' we'll no' be aboot tae cramp yer style, more like!"

"You boys, ye've minds like a burst sewer. Just you keep oota trouble, is all ah'm sayin'. Ah'll no' be there tae keep an eye on youse, so ye better be oan yer best behaviour."

The rumble of the bus sounded outside, and the Beaters piled out. Willie went to see them off.

"They're all yours, Grallocher, see'n bring them back in the same state you got them."

"If these boil-infested wee arse-scratchers were all mine, MacBog, I'd drive over the nearest cliff."

Willie watched as the bus ground off through the trees, the mingled odours of burnt oil and cheap after-shave hanging heavy in the evening air.

The bus trundled along Inverdruel's main street, slowing down and squealing to a halt at the crossroads beside the village hall, from which the members of the W.R.I. were just beginning to emerge after a fascinating lecture and slide-show given by the local minister on the subject of the varied wildlife to be found around Inverdruel. Perhaps if Willie had been on the bus, disaster might have been averted - the deterrent effect of a timely knuckle on the ear may have made all the difference. But Willie was several miles away, and involved in gentler pursuits.

Attracted by the muffled sound of primeval hooting, the members of the W.R.I., including the chairwoman, Maud Manley-Buttocks, turned and stared across the road. After a few seconds of incomprehension, they blanched, they gasped, they recoiled in horror at the array of squashed noses, flattened lips and other pallid physiognomical distortions pressing against the windows of the bus, only feet away from them. Like a tortoise sensing danger, Grallocher slid down in his seat so that his jacket collar rose up round his ears, then, deciding in a flash that the possibility of being crushed by a juggernaut was better than the certainty of being handbagged to death by the W.R.I., he jammed his foot down hard on the accelerator and the bus shot off with its heaving cargo of gargoyles.

Indelibly impressed on the collective consciousness of the Inverdruel W.R.I. was the receding vision of the back of the bus, its small oval window completely filled by four off-white buttocks.

The Beaters tumbled boisterously into the bar, some still adjusting their dress. Andromeda was deep in conversation with Aloysius Flannelly and, over in the alcove, Lavinia Hathaway sat on a low stool by the fire, displaying her marvellous poise. Stratford stood at the bar, one finger raised in the air.

"In the immortal words of Keats – 'O for a draught of vintage! that hath been cooled a long age in the deep delve'd earth, tasting of Flora and the country green, Dance, and Provençal song, and sunburnt mirth! O for a beaker full of the warm South, full of the true, the blushful Hippocrene'."

"Would that be another glass of the house red, sir?" enquired Andromeda, an edge to her voice.

"Yes, m'dear, you surmise correctly."

"Ah'll try a pint o' that" said a Beater.

"Hi, boys!" beamed Andromeda. "Where's Willie?"

There was an awkward silence. Andromeda looked at them, staring from one to another.

"Well? What've you done with ma boy?"

"Eh, he's got a cold, Andromeda; aye, he caught a nasty chill."

Aloysius chuckled.

"Sure then, boys, that must've been the kiss o' life the Major's daughter was after givin' him down by the stream the other day! I'd say he had a high temperature, right enough. I'd say it would've blown the top off any thermometer!"

Slowly, a cold, hard look came into Andromeda's eyes.

"If it's all right with you, Mr Flannelly ... Aloysius ... I've changed my mind. I think I'll accept that drink from you after all – and make it a double."

The Beaters grabbed their pints and scuttled across to the far side of the bar.

"Christ, what'll we do? She knows! Willie's a dead man! Who's gonny tell 'im?"

They stared at each other.

"Maybe we could just, sort of ... drop a hint?"

Don't be fucking stupid! How d'ye drop a hint tae a boy that his newly-ex-girlfriend's plannin' tae rip off his balls an' jump up'n doon on them!"

"Aye, ah s'pose. Mebbe best no tae mention it, eh?"

"Right. No point upsettin' 'im."

"Aye - he'd only worry. Might as well let 'im enjoy his last few days."

As the Beaters huddled round their pints, trying to avoid eye contact with Andromeda, who was now laughing loudly at all of Aloysius's jokes, they gradually became aware that they were being talked about.

"I say, Strattie, you could be right, you know ... a simply super idea ... "

" ... and look at that small one, the one with the odd sleeve. Did you ever see anything more ... misérable ... in your life!"

"Yes, yes! They would be perfect, I'm sure of it. Modern proletarian vernacular giving contemporary resonance and a cutting edge to a classic piece!"

"Hm, they would certainly bring a gritty realism to the production, enhance its essential dichotomy."

The Beaters listened attentively, staring at one another in incomprehension.

Stratford continued, "How should we approach them, though? They are rather ... rough."

Lavinia's perfect vowels floated across the bar. "Perhaps, Strattie ... if you offered them ... a drink?"

The Beaters froze. Through the cloud of verbal static they were beginning to pick up words they understood. Words like "offer" and "drink."

"I say, you chaps" called Stratford, hesitantly.

The Beaters' heads turned, as one.

"Could I possibly interest you ... in a drink?"

The alcove was instantly mobbed by a scrum of "chaps" whose interest in drink was keen, all expressing their particular preferences, some expressing several preferences.

By the time Stratford's wallet, lighter and slimmer, was returned to its place of rest he had gained the Beaters' full attention.

"I have a proposition for you fellows. I understand that, shortly, when the season ends, you will become unemployed? Well, I propose to offer you positions as extras for the crowd scenes in my forthcoming production ... "

"Is there naked wimmen in it?"

"No, I'm afraid not ... in my forthcoming London production of 'Les Misérables' ... "

"London? But that's in England!"

"Quite so, quite so - all reasonable expenses will be covered. You shall be in my employ until the production has finished its run, at which time you will be free to return home."

"Is it good wages?"

"You would be paid the standard rates."

"We'd take less if there was naked wimmen!"

"Dreadfully sorry, old chap, there are definitely no naked women."

"Hm - we'll huv tae speak tae oor agent."

"Your agent? you have an agent?"

"Aye. Willie. He's oor agent. He handles all oor financial affairs, ye know."

"Aye, he might even insist on naked wimmen. Then again, come tae think on it, he might huv other things on his mind ... "

"OK, boys, hands up them that want a job wi' Mr Hathaway here, and is in favour of anither pint!"

"Aye, that looks unanimous. Anither pint fur yer extras, Mr Hathaway?"

Stratford sighed heavily, and reached for his wallet.

The bus dipped and swayed, Grallocher the unlikely coxswain of the wheeled lifeboat which conveyed the survivors away from the alcoholic maelstrom of Inverdruel Hotel and landed them, bleary-eyed and bladder-wracked, back at the Bothy, high-tide mark for the night.

The optimists scuttled, bow-legged, towards the toilet, where a tight-lipped tussle ensued, their dangerously swollen bladders precluding the use of full-blown violence. The realists fanned out into the rhododendrons which, fortunately, thrive in acid soil It was one of the realists who, while in the process of shaking the drips off, spotted the ladder propped against the wall beneath Cynthia's window at the back of the Lodge. Her room was in darkness.

When Willie strode into the cook-house the next day he was puzzled at first. It was not like the Beaters to be whistling on a Sunday morning. He recognised several of the tunes, old favourites such as 'Climbing the Stairway to Heaven' and 'When I'm Cleaning Windows' before their significance dawned on him.

"Aye, boys, very funny! Very droll!" He swiftly changed the subject. "An' whit wis the crack in Inverdruel? Good time had by all?"

The Beaters related at length and enthusiastically, rather too enthusiastically, the story of Stratford Hathaway's offer of employment at the end of the season.

"Ah'm right pleased for ye, boys, the job an' that, you should go fur it, nuthin' tae lose, but ... you little basturds ur hidin' somethin'. Ah c'n tell!"

The Beaters looked at one another, desperately hoping for inspiration.

"We bared wur arses!"

"Aye, that's it, Willie! We mooned at the W.R.I. wifies comin' oot'a the Hall!"

"An' made horrible faces at them, an' aw!"

"Christ!" said Willie, "how could they tell which wuz an arse an' which wuz a face? Ah warned youse tae behave yersels, ye stupit little fuckers. Ye've probably no heard the end o' this, ye know. Them wimmen frae the W.R.I. can be bloody dangerous, specially in large numbers. So is that it? Ye've nuthin' more tae tell me?"

The Beaters shook their heads vigorously. Willie gave them a long, hard look.

CHAPTER 19

"HEATHENS!"

The Reverend Hector Brimstone smote the lectern a mighty blow with his clenched fist.

"GODLESS ... BLASPHEMOUS ... HEATHENS!"

The words rolled around the small church, booming off the thick walls, bouncing against each other and bludgeoning the blackened souls of the perspiring, mint-sucking sinners packed beneath him in the hard, buttock-buffed pews.

Throughout the week, as the inhabitants of Inverdruel went about their sinful lives, the Wrath of the Lord slowly built up and was stored in the small church which squatted, grey and unadorned, on a hillock outside the village. Its walls were low and thick, built to withstand the pressure of a week's supply of Inverdruel's sins. A scatter of lichen-covered gravestones surrounded it, poking through the sparse, sheep-cropped grass like crooked teeth, permanent reminders of the mortality of man and the importance of regular dental care.

Every Sunday, at 11.30am precisely, the Reverend Hector Brimstone ascended the pulpit steps with heavy tread, and for the next hour and fifteen minutes became a veritable conduit for the Wrath of the Lord. The souls of Inverdruel's sinners were washed clean by the pounding waves of his oratory, the astringent lash of his tongue reaching into even the most awkward crevices.

"Fornicators! Despoilers of Virtue! Brawlers! Imbibers!

Again he pounded the lectern, again the ranks of sinners quailed beneath the flail of his righteous indignation. Gripping the pulpit-rail tightly, he leaned forward. In their pews, the sinners shrank back. The minister's voice dropped ominously.

"We are all guilty in the eyes of the Lord, are we not? For our sins, however, there can be redemption. But into our midst have come devils for whom there can be NO redemption." His voice began to rise again.

"Yes, I say unto you, the Fornicators, the Despoilers of Virtue, the Brawlers, the Imbibers - they are abominations in the eyes of the Lord! Like the worm in the apple these sons of Satan gnaw at our vitals! Now they have sunk to the lowest depths of depravity. They have bared their heathen parts in the sight of God-fearing members of this congregation!" He paused, his piercing eyes roving slowly along the serried ranks of the sinful. Then, in a low voice, he continued:

"I am distressed to note that several members of the W.R.I. have not yet recovered sufficiently to attend today's service!"

Pausing, he drew himself up and, in a voice that shook the very rafters, he roared:

"THE DAYS OF PUNISHMENT HAVE COME! THE DAYS OF RECOMPENSE HAVE COME!"

He glared at the congregation, and slowly hissed "Who will rid us of these turbulent pests ... ?"

In the silence that followed you could have heard a peppermint drop ...

The congregation was bottle-necked, those at the back pressing determinedly forward, those at the front shuffling towards the narrow arched doorway, every inch gained a small triumph. One at a time they popped out, blinking, into the sunlight, stretching, loosening their ties and inhaling great lungfuls of God's fresh air.

"Minister was in fine form today" said one, removing a wad of cotton wool from each ear.

"Aye", said his companion. "Thank God ah'm no' a sinner!"

In the churchyard small knots of women formed and reformed, chattering like sparrows and carefully eyeing up each other's hats. By the door of the church a cohort of grim-faced W.R.I. matrons huddled round Maud Manley-Buttocks, listening intently as she appeared to be giving instructions. The conversation came to an end and they nodded, tight-lipped, as if in agreement.

" ... and the code-word" said Maud Manley-Buttocks, "will be 'Geronimo'!"

CHAPTER 20

When the Beaters returned from the day's shooting there was an unpleasant surprise waiting for them. A police car was parked beside the Bothy and Constable McNab, who represented the forces of law and order in Inverdruel, was perched on the bonnet, his hat pushed well back on his head, tie loosened and the glowing stub of a hand-rolled cigarette pinched between thumb and forefinger. It was obviously an official visit.

As the Beaters tumbled from their trailer McNab climbed down stiffly from the bonnet of his car, tugging at the seat of his trousers. He flicked his cigarette-end into the bushes and crooked his finger.

"A word, lads!"

The Beaters shuffled over, looking incredibly furtive.

"It wisnae us!"

"Ah've received reports" he said, ignoring the case for the defence, "of a severe outbreak of Multiple Indecent Exposure ... "

"Ye've no proof!"

"Don't give me that! Who else would be drivin' through Inverdruel in a bus on a Saturday night with their trousers round their ankles?"

Grallocher was still standing anxiously beside the Land Rover. He coughed pointedly.

"OK, Grallocher" said McNab, "this doesn't concern you; you can go."

"A bit o' police brutality" Grallocher muttered to the Beaters as he passed, "that'll fix you, you perverted little bastards" and, looking extremely relieved, he headed off towards the Lodge.

"So, urr ye gonny hold an identity parade then?" demanded a Beater. "Make us all bend over so they wimmen can point oot the suspects?"

There was a sudden loud crack, and the Beater doubled up, clutching his ear.

"Don't you be a cheeky wee shit" growled Willie.

Constable McNab looked alarmed.

115

"It's OK, Willie, they're not goin' to be charged. Mrs Manley-Buttocks is in a dodgy position. She's the big cheese at the W.R.I. right enough, but with her husband bein' this lot's employer ... an, besides, they don't want is splashed all over the 'Bugle'. Could be embarrassin'. Mrs Manley-Buttocks seems to think the W.R.I. are goin' to sort this one out themselves."

"Hm" said Willie, looking thoughtful. "But whit the hell can the W.R.I. do? Stone us tae death wi' home-bakes?"

Constable McNab raised a sardonic eyebrow.

"Ma wife's in the W.R.I." he said. "Those home-bakes can be deadly. Anyway, Willie, ah'm just warnin' you - there's somethin' in the wind. AND ... no more bare arses, eh?"

He was just about to climb into his car when there was a puttering noise and a Reliant three-wheeler appeared, heading up the drive.

"Christ!" spat Constable McNab. "Speak o' the devil. It's that bastard McCronnicle!"

The three-wheeler rolled to a stop and Scoop McCronnicle leapt out like an uncoiled spring. He reached back into the car for his trilby, the one with the ticket in the hat-band saying "PRESS", then strode up in a brisk, no-nonsense manner, whipping a notebook from his back pocket and licking his pencil as he approached.

"Did they resist arrest, Constable?"

"No" replied McNab in a tired voice.

"Suspects ... Evade ... Police ... Dragnet" wrote Scoop, mouthing the words.

"Dragnet, McCronnicle?" enquired McNab sourly. " ... a one-man ... dragnet?"

A look of impatience flitted across Scoop's features as he scored out a couple of sentences.

"Police ... Remain ... Tight ... Lipped" he wrote.

"I can inform you that charges are not being pressed" said the constable with a cold smile. As he climbed into his car he turned to the Beaters.

"A word of advice, lads" he said, " ... never talk to the press."

As he disappeared down the drive, Scoop turned to the Beaters.

"OK, boys" he said briskly, "on the evening in question, what exactly happened?"

"Fuck off!"

Scoop stepped back, startled at the menace implicit in the words.

"Beaters Deny Involvement in Bared Bottom Bust-Up" he scribbled quickly, then scrambled into his three-wheeler and chugged away at speed, before he became a War Correspondent.

CHAPTER 21

"Come on, you drippy-nosed wee arseholes" roared Grallocher, "put a bloody spurt on!"

It was the last shooting day of the week and the Beaters climbed slowly out of the trailer, stiff and aching after a particularly bone-jarring trip into the hills. By this stage of the season they had become totally impervious to Grallocher's ranting abuse. They stood around, stretching and yawning and scratching their bottoms, taking final drags on cigarettes before extinguishing them and tucking them behind their ears. With only a token amount of elbowing and jostling they fell into rough formation behind Willie and waited for the whistle. Soon they heard the long, shrill peep, and they began to scuttle up the rise. Almost immediately there was a single shot, and what sounded like a scream in the distance.

"Trigger-happy basturds" grumbled a Beater, then they were over the rise and pounding across the open ground. They were almost half way over the hill when their headlong career began to falter. They slowed, then stopped, staring around in confusion. The only sound which broke the unnerving silence was their own rasping breath. Slowly, they realised that no-one was shooting at them.

"Look!" One of the Beaters pointed across the hill. "Somethin's up."

The Guests had risen to their feet and appeared to be clustered round a figure on the ground. The Beaters shrugged.

"Better take a wander over an' see whit's up?"

As they trudged through the heather one of them imitated the Major's clipped tones:

"Be careful men! It could be a ruse. They're fiendish cunning, these cheps!"

"Aye, mebbe we better wave a piece o' white cloth!"

"Ah've a hankie here."

One of the Beaters hauled a crumpled, encrusted piece of rag from his pocket. It made crackling noises as he tried to open it.

"Jesus Christ! Put that away before it bites somebody!"

"Fuck me, it's the Major!"

The Guests were gathered round the prostrate body of Manley-Buttocks, who lay face-down in the heather, groaning loudly. Grallocher appeared to be investigating his hindquarters. The Beaters crowded round, pushing between the white-faced Guests for a better view.

"C'mon, let us through - we're ghouls."

"What's up Doc?" one of them inquired brightly of Grallocher. He looked up and glared.

"Bugger off, you snot-faced wee scumbags! Go on, get out of it!"

"Tisk, tisk, Grallocher, ah'm no impressed wi' yer bedside manner."

"Bugger off!" he roared.

The Beater retreated a few feet.

"Not a nice man at all", he muttered in injured tones.

Grallocher had returned his attentions to the Major, whose posterior was a sticky mess of tattered, blood-soaked tweed.

"Nothing for it, sur, I'll go back just now with the Beaters and I'll phone McLush from the Lodge. You'll have to come down in one of the Land Rovers with the Guests.

"Psssst! Brent! Whit happened?"

Brent came over and joined the Beaters. It transpired that, when the Major had blown his whistle for the start of the run, Widgery-Sprockett had struggled to his feet, shouted "Damn' Boche!", and blasted both barrels into the Major's backside from a range of about twenty yards. Had it not been for the thickness of the tweed material in the seat of the Major's plus-fours, he would have been more seriously injured. As it was, his bottom was not a pretty sight.

The Beaters climbed into their trailer, hearing the Major's agonised cries echoing distantly as the Guests attempted to manhandle him into a Land Rover. Grallocher crashed the gears, and they set off with a sudden lurch, immediately bouncing into a pothole in the track. Normally they would have cursed Grallocher horribly, but this time they looked back towards the Guests and grinned happily.

The Beaters had never seen the Doctor so bad. He had had to be assisted from his car, and now he leaned against it, hiccupping and sighing heavily. Jim remained in the passenger seat. He had the look about him of a dog who had lost all faith in human nature. The Beaters opened the door and tried to coax him out, but he stared straight ahead, refusing to move. He was no longer man's best friend.

"Poor basturd, eh."

"Lissen" suggested a Beater, "why not take him roon' tae see that poodle-thing in the kennels? It's anither dug - it might cheer him up."

"Good idea, on ye go then."

"C'mon, Jim, c'mon, come an' see this lovely dug."

Jim tried to resist. After the episode with the toffee, who knew what fresh ordeals his tormentors had lined up for him? But several hands sought out the collar under his matted hair, and he was dragged ignominiously from the car. He looked up, his eyes full of pleading, but to no avail. He briefly tried to make a stand by straightening his legs, but he started to get friction burns on his paws.

When the Beaters got Jim manhandled round to the kennels, Fluffles, aroused by all the commotion, was standing on her hind legs, her paws on the low concrete wall at the base of the railings.

"Look, Jim - a dug! An' it's even got a ribbon on its heid!"

They loosened their hold on Jim and stood back.

"He likes it. Look, he's waggin' his tail!"

Yes, Jim WAS wagging his tail. He knew there had to be a catch - there just had to be. But who cared!

Suddenly, the distant rumble of engines could be heard. The Guests were back.

"In ye go, Jim, an' say 'hello' tae the nice dug. We'll come back fur ye in a few minutes ... ", and the iron-barred gate clanged shut behind him.

The Beaters raced round to the front of the Lodge. The Major was bent over the bonnet of a Land Rover, surrounded by anxious-looking Guests.

"Sorry we took so long, Doctor" Stratford was saying, "had to take it very easy. The man is in terrible pain."

The Doctor leaned over and pressed his finger against a piece of bloody tweed. The Major screamed.

"Hem ... royds! Wurss case f'evr seen."

Grallocher stared incredulously at the Doctor.

"Haemorrhoids?" he roared, ignoring the startled Guests.

"Haemorrhoids! You stupid old bastard! The man's been shot!"

"Oh!" The Doctor too looked startled.

"M'sdyag ... Miss dyag ... nosis" he muttered, "c'd happen't ... anyone."

The Doctor bent down and peered again at the Major's bottom.

"Thish man needsh 'orse ... piddle" he declared.

"Horse piddle?" muttered a Beater, his face screwed up with incomprehension.

"It'll be wan o' they old countryside cures" one of the others explained. "Apply horse-piss tae affected parts twice daily ... somethin' like that."

"Grall ... cher!" ordered the Doctor, asserting his authority now, as a trained medical practitioner, "phone f'r 'namnilence 'meedly, ther'sh ... good chap.

"JIM! Whersh ... dam' ... dog?"

The Beaters looked at one another, and kept quiet.

"Bloody dog, g'n all t'hell reshen'ly", and the Doctor wavered back to the car to collect the bag himself, then set off in mazy pursuit of Grallocher and the Guests, who were assisting the Major towards the Lodge. The Major was taking very small steps, and groaning.

When the Doctor emerged about fifteen minutes later, the Beaters were still hanging around.

"Did ye huv tae ampyitate his arse, Doctor?"

"Is it gonny be wan o' they transplants? Grallocher's offered tae donate his face."

"Not s'bad shlooks, lads. 'Njection, 'stract'a pellets, week'n 'orse ... piddle. Be right's rain!"

The Doctor stopped and stared around, a puzzled look on his face.

"Whersh ma bloody dog?"

"It's OK, Doc, no sweat, ah'll jist nip roon' an' get 'im. He's been socialisin'." The Beater sprinted off.

A couple of minutes later he reappeared round the corner of the Lodge. He was walking backwards, crouched down, and making encouraging noises. Jim slowly came into view. He took a couple of steps forwards, then lurched off to one side before straightening up and taking a few wobbling steps forward again.

"Christ!" said a Beater. "He's doin' an impression o' the Doctor! Bloody brilliant! He could get ontae 'That's Life'!"

But, as Jim zig-zagged towards them, the Beaters realised that he was not actually acting. His breath came in great rasping sobs, his sides heaved, his bloodshot eyes bulged wildly, and his tongue hung out.

"Huv you been makin' him do press-ups or somethin'? He's totally knackered!"

"That's the way ah found 'im!" declared the Beater indignantly. "He wuz lyin' on the ground beside that poodle-thing, blawin' an' puffin' like a pensioner at a disco. Ah even hud tae help him tae his feet!"

By now Jim had made it as far as the passenger door, where he stopped, wheezing and panting.

"C'mon you ... shtupit an'mal!" shouted the Doctor. The Beaters gathered round and helped Jim into the car. One of them fished in his pocket and produced a gnarled, grey object. He held it out.

"Here ye go, Jim. T'make up fur the toffee. Wan o' Cook's doughballs. Ah've been keepin' it fur ye."

Jim sniffed it suspiciously, obviously expecting it to be booby-trapped, then, throwing caution to the winds he took it gingerly between his teeth.

As the Doctor's car juddered off down the drive, Jim looked back over his shoulder, his brown eyes moist with gratitude, the doughball clamped firmly between his jaws. It was far too precious to eat immediately. He would take it home and bury it.

About an hour later the ambulance arrived at the Lodge. The Beaters gathered outside the Bothy to spectate. After several minutes the main door opened and two ambulance men appeared, manoeuvring cautiously down the steps with a stretcher. The Major lay on it, face down, one arm dangling from either side. He was mumbling incoherently - evidently Doctor McLush's painkillers were taking effect. A bloodstained pile of knotted bandages lay over his rear, and another length of bandage trailed along the ground. It looked as if the Doctor had tried to apply a tourniquet to the Major's bottom, but it had slipped off.

"Whit a bloody mess" muttered a Beater approvingly.

"Looks like a double puddin' supper, heavy on the tomato sauce."

As the ambulance began to move slowly off down the drive, one of the Beaters whipped off his woolly bonnet, clasped it to his chest and saluted stiffly.

The ambulance was just rounding the first bend when it swerved suddenly, with a squeal of brakes. A muffled thump and a cry came from inside, as if something heavy had crashed to the floor. Rocking violently, a Reliant three-wheeler swerved past it and, heeling over at an alarming angle, completed a tight U-turn in front of the Lodge.

Scoop McCronnicle had spotted the ambulance speeding through Inverdruel and, with his uncanny nose for a story, had set off in pursuit.

He kept the engine running, his recent interview with the Beaters still fresh in his mind. Winding the window down a couple of inches, he peered out warily at the jostling crowd who had surrounded his three-wheeler. The look of anxiety on his face slowly gave way to one of delight when he realised that they were not actually threatening him, but were vying with each other to be interviewed! The details that poured out were so blood-curdling and graphic that, at one stage, his pencil broke and a fist-fight broke out among the Beaters while he re-sharpened it.

Finally, he puttered off, bearing several cans of beer and a half bottle of whisky which the Beaters had pressed on him, and with cries of "Good man, Scoop!" ringing in his ears.

'ESTATE BOSS IN SHOTGUN DRAMA - EXCLUSIVE!'

Hmm - he liked the sound of that ... But it could be improved.

CHAPTER 22

Saturday night had come round again and the Beaters were completing the final stages of the primping process when Willie came into the Bothy. He was wearing his new jeans and his Fair Isle jersey. The Beaters stared.

"No need fur the big round eyes, boys, ye've seen ma good duds before."

"It's no' that, Willie - just wondered, were ye goin' somewhere?"

"Aye. After last week's disgustin' behaviour from you basturds in Inverdruel ah thought ah better go along an' ride shotgun, keep you oota trouble. An' ah thought as well ah'd mebbe better huv a wee word wi' Andromeda, put her in the picture, ye know, aboot Cynthia'n me - sorta break it gently."

The Beaters shuddered inwardly. They suspected Andromeda would not be breaking anything gently. Multiple fractures would be a safer bet. Probably with massive blood loss.

There was a rumble outside, and a squeal of brakes.

"Ah, boys, that will be our carriage!"

They piled out of the Bothy and onto the bus, scuffling briefly over the choicest seats, though it was difficult to scuffle properly without messing up your hair.

"Inverdruel Hotel, my good man, and don't spare the horses!"

"Aye, pit yer foot doon, Grallocher, there's a chap, ah've a couple o' starlets waitin' fur me!"

"Only two?" enquired his companion.

"Aye, ah'm cuttin' back. Ah went fur a sperm count the other day an' the doctor niver even got intae double figures. 'Go easy on the starlets' he said."

Grallocher squinted into the rear-view mirror, his face twisted with contempt.

"Bloody fairies! Bring back National Service!", and he released the clutch venomously.

There was a strange atmosphere on the bus. On the Inverdruel trip there was always a heady buzz of excitement, but on this occasion there was a manic intensity about the banter, an edge of hysteria to the laughter which Willie, sitting in their midst joking and playfully knuckling heads, seemed quite unaware of.

There was a nervous cheer as twinkling lights appeared in the distance. Like an asteroid speeding on a direct collision course with planet Earth, the bus rumbled down the hill towards Inverdruel, and the first houses on the outskirts of the village began to slip past ...

"WHAT THE ... !" Grallocher stood on the brakes. The bus screeched to a juddering halt in an acrid cloud of burnt rubber. The Beaters were hurled around, several thrown from their seats.

"Stepped right out in front of me!" roared Grallocher, pounding his clenched fists on the steering wheel. The Beaters slowly picked themselves up, dazed and disorientated. They stared around. It was almost dark, but in the murky light of the street lamps they could see that they were stopped almost level with the Village Hall. The street was deserted apart from a woman slowly pushing a wheelchair across the road. In the wheelchair sat a hunched figure.

"Bloody cripples" snarled Grallocher, "come on, get a bloody move on!"

The silence was broken only by a faint, rhythmic squeak, which seemed to come from the wheelchair as it crossed the road in front of the bus. There was something ... unnerving about it

The hairs on the backs of the Beaters' necks began to prickle ...

"GERONIMO!"

Their blood froze. They recognised that terrible cry. Grallocher gasped as the invalid threw off her tartan blanket and sprang from the wheelchair. The Beaters saw the menacing glint of bifocals, those awful flashing eyes ...

"It's the Beast!"

Suddenly, the door of the Hall burst open and a phalanx of W.R.I. matrons poured down the steps. Mrs Brimstone, the minister's wife, was in the vanguard, waving a placard.

"Mothers Against Sin and Hooliganism" it screamed, in neat letters.

Like a rabbit caught in the glare of car headlights, Grallocher froze. He sat motionless, staring unblinking into the far distance, hands locked round the steering wheel. The bag-swinging, umbrella-brandishing, brogue-clad Amazons blitzkrieged their way onto the bus and stormed up the aisle.

"The Lord is with us!" cried Mrs Brimstone.

"Get their trousers off!" cried Maud Manley-Buttocks, her eyes flashing terribly.

Under the onslaught the stunned Beaters were driven back, cowering, towards the rear of the bus.

"Heathens!" cried one woman.

"Fornicators!" cried another, as they laid about them with handbags and dealt mighty blows with furled umbrellas. One brandished a knitting needle (No 2 size), jabbing and thrusting like Errol Flynn in his heyday. Another, in flagrant defiance of the Geneva Arms Convention, was lashing out with a rolled up copy of "The People's Friend."

"The emergency exit! The emergency exit!" the desperate cry rose above the hubbub. The door swung open with a crash and, like corks from a bottle, Beaters popped out, some falling together in a tangle of arms and legs, others hitting the ground running.

The broken rabble scuttered down the street, pursued briefly by a posse of hefty matrons but, fortunately, years spent sampling home-baked scones, buns and shortbread in W.R.I. competitions had played havoc with their sprinting abilities.

"Oh mammy!" gasped a breathless Beater, when they finally managed to regroup at a safe distance, "ah thought ah'd died an' gone tae hell!"

"Urr we safe? They'll mebbe still come after us."

"Naw, it's OK" said Willie, "they'll hardly follow us intae a pub. They've prob'ly gone back tae the Hall tae knit toilet-roll covers or somethin'. But please, please, boys, frae now on - no more bare arses, eh? It's jist no' worth it."

They heard the noise of an approaching vehicle, the sound overlaid by the dull boom of loud rock music. As they turned round the police car drew to a halt beside them, the music becoming a deafening blast as PC McNab wound down the window. He reached over and turned down the volume on his radio.

"Aye, lads" he snorted cheerfully, "looks like a buildin' fell on ye!"

"Lissen, Constable" said Willie, "next time these boys go moonin' do me a favour - jist lock the little basturds up in a nice safe cell."

"Aye, it's a big problem nowadays" continued McNab, "vigilante groups handin' out rough justice. And the thing is, you can never catch them at it! Anyway, ah'm off duty now, so ah'm away home to get a blow by blow account from the wife. See you, lads!" and, grinning hugely, he pushed his cap to the back of his head, turned the volume on the radio back up and roared off down the street.

"Christ! Let's go an' get oorsel's a nice, quiet pint" said Willie.

As they approached the Hotel the Beaters began to hold back.

"Whit's up wi' youse?" asked Willie, looking round at them.

The Beaters shuffled and avoided his gaze.
"Well, Willie ... it's Andromeda."
"Whit aboot Andromeda?"
"Well, you said you wuz gonny ... mention to her ... aboot Cynthia ... ?"

"Aye, well? Ah'll huv tae tell her some time. So whit's yer problem?"

"We jist thought ... it'd be better if we waited oot here. Jist for a couple o' minutes. So's we don't cramp yer style. Ye know whit wimmen urr like."

"Ach, me'n Andromeda'll discuss this like adults. Ah'll break it to her gentle."

"Aye, but, all the same, can we jist wait here a couple o' minutes? While ye do the business?"

"Well, suit yersel's boys."

The Beaters watched glumly as Willie strode towards the bar. As the door swung closed behind him, they rushed to the window, jostling for position, noses pressed against the glass.

The atmosphere in the bar was quiet and peaceful as Willie entered. In the corner the television burbled away, watched intently by the Oldest Inhabitant, who fancied the newscaster in spite of his vermilion features. Lavinia and Stratford Hathaway sat in the alcove and, among the few drinkers at the bar, Aloysius Flannelly was engaged in deep conversation with Andromeda. Over in the far corner the Inverdruel Rockettes were assembling their equipment in readiness for a session later in the evening.

Willie walked up to the counter.

"Pint o' lager" he said, and smiled winningly at Andromeda.

"I'll just be a minute, Aloysius."

She patted his hand, then turned towards Willie. There were a few seconds of silence.

"A pint of lager?" she said, quietly.

Slowly she began to untie her apron. Willie looked at her, still smiling.

"A ... PINT ... OF ... LAGER!"

She loosened her apron and flung it on the counter. Outside, the Beaters groaned and covered their eyes. There was total silence in the bar now, as Andromeda walked slowly round from behind the counter. Alarm bells had begun to trill wildly in Willie's brain, but the message had not yet reached his facial muscles. The smile was still there.

"You dirty, rotten, two-timin' scumbag!" she hissed. There was a loud smack as her podgy hand bounced off the side of Willie's face.

"But ... Andromeda ... "

"You twisted, lyin', cheatin' rat!"

With a dull thud her fist sank into Willie's stomach. He doubled up, winded.

Aloysius watched in admiration. He had done a bit of amateur boxing in his time and he recognised class when he saw it.

"God love ye, girleen" he muttered, "ye've a divil of a jab on you!"

" ... slimy, skulkin', two-faced low-life ... "

Andromeda had Willie in a powerful head-lock now and she aimed a blow at his face with her free hand.

"Uuuuurrgh!" cried Willie in a muffled voice, "ah c'n explain, ah c'n ... "

His voice tailed into a strangled squawk as another blow sailed into his face.

" ... deceivin', underhanded, two-timin' toad!"

Andromeda dragged Willie round the bar, still gripping him in a ferocious head-lock.

"Heaven has no rage like love to hatred turned" intoned Stratford Hathaway from the safety of the alcove. Lavinia's face was covered by her hands, but she watched the struggle through the gaps between her fingers.

"Give me a break, Andromeda. Ah've had enough", mumbled Willie desperately.

"Have ye now?" said Andromeda, and once more her podgy fist smacked into his face.

" ... sneaky, shameless, double-crossin' shit", and she finally released her hold on Willie, who sank to his knees, gasping and clutching his throat. His nose looked like a burst tomato.

Aloysius dashed over and raised Andromeda's arm.

"Technical knockout!" he declared, and escorted her gently back to the bar.

"What a woman!" he said, his face lit up with admiration. "What a woman!"

He returned to Willie, and helped him slowly to his feet.

"Good man yourself. Bejasus, but she's not a girl to be messin' with!"

As Willie made his way unsteadily towards the door the theme music from the film 'Rocky' suddenly reverberated around the bar. Willie turned and glared at the Rockettes.

"Very funny! Very fucking funny!"

"How'd ye get on, Willie?" asked a Beater, politely.

"Talked it over like adults, didn't we", mumbled Willie through thickening lips. The Beaters shuffled and looked at one another awkwardly.

"So whit's wur next move? We canny stand aboot here aw night."

"Where the hell's oor transport?"

At that moment the bus appeared. It edged slowly round the corner, crawled towards them, and jolted suddenly to a stop. Grallocher's fists were clenched tightly round the steering wheel. A small muscle in his face twitched spasmodically. He was in a state of considerable shock. On his neck was a large purple love-bite. It looked to have been freshly inflicted. One of the Beaters nudged his neighbour. With a nod of his head he indicated Grallocher:

"Ah've read aboot that in 'The Bugle', ye know. It's the 'in' thing nowadays. They're aw at it."

"Whit's that?"

"Older folk. Havin' a active sex-life."

A barely perceptible tremor ran through Grallocher's whole body.

"Lissen, boys" said Willie, "ah think we've had enough fur wan night. How about we pit oor beer money in a kitty an' a couple o' you lads nip in an' get a huge carry-oot, an' we'll head fur home an' huv a wee consolation back at the Bothy?"

As two volunteers cautiously entered the bar, holding out fistfuls of notes to indicate their peaceful intentions, the theme music from 'Rocky' drifted through the open door and faded again as it swung shut behind them.

"Basturds" muttered Willie.

Once they were back in the Bothy the Beaters' spirits began to lift. They were on home ground now, and could lick the physical and psychological wounds inflicted by the W.R.I. They dragged chairs into a rough semi-circle around the stove, which was prodded and poked till it gave off a shimmering heat. One of the tables groaned under a spectacular assortment of cans and bottles which gleamed seductively in the orange glow. To the accompaniment of clinking glass, and the staccato pop and hiss of opened beer cans, the jokes and laughter grew ever louder.

The Bothy door opened and Willie appeared with Cynthia.

"Aha! It's Snow White come tae see her dwarfs! An' look! She's brought the Creature frae the Black Lagoon!"

The low light from the stove highlighted Willie's bumps and bruises.

The Beaters made a space for Cynthia.

"Grab a seat, gorgeous!"

"Thanks, boys. I didn't realise there was going to be a party tonight."

"Aye, it's tae celebrate Willie an' Andromeda reachin' an ... understandin'."

"Yes" said Cynthia, "Willie was trying to explain what happened: apparently Andromeda was very sympathetic, but the story seemed a bit confused."

"Ah, it's OK, Cynth, we'll tell ye all aboot it!"

Willie looked daggers at the speaker who, newly emboldened by drink and an enthusiastic audience, pretended not to notice.

"Well" he said, "Andromeda broke it off. But, not to worry, Cynthia, plastic surgeons can perform miracles nowadays."

The Beaters roared with laughter, while Willie muttered darkly.

"Aye, it wuz wan hell o' a night" continued the Beater. "First yer mother an' a bunch o' her W.R.I. heavies ambushed us oan the bus an' gave us a terrible doin'. Ah'm tellin' ye, the streets nowadays jist urnae safe. We live in awful times, so we do."

"Yes" said Cynthia, "Willie told me how he got his face all bruised, trying to save you ... "

There were several seconds of silence.

" ... He told you WHAT?" gasped a Beater incredulously.

"JESUS CHRIST!" roared Willie, dabbing whisky from a cut on his swollen lip, "that bloody stings!"

"Anyway" continued the Beater, "tae get on wi' the story, the TRUE story, that is - ah wuz studyin' Andromeda's body language, ye know, when hur an' Willie was reachin' their understandin'? Mebbe ah wuz readin' the signs wrong, but ah did get the vague feelin' that she wuz a bit sniffy."

"Did you notice that as well?" interrupted another Beater. "Me too. Ah thought, at one stage, ah could detect negative vibrations. A breakdown in communications, even."

The other Beaters nodded in delighted agreement.

"An' that last smack she gave him - right in the gob, a real beauty ... !"

"She hit him!" exclaimed Cynthia, looking round at Willie, wide-eyed. "You never told me that Andromeda hit you!"

"It wuz like edited highlights o' the Massacre o' Glencoe!" continued the Beater, enthusiastically, "Wi' action replays!"

"Well, well, well" said Cynthia, turning again to face Willie, who sat hunched beside her, staring fixedly into his glass.

"Aw, c'mon, doll, geez a break" he muttered. His swollen face twisted into an embarrassed grin, "an' mebbe a straw tae suck this bloody whisky through, eh ... ?

CHAPTER 23

Next morning those Beaters who could face breakfast made their way across to the cookhouse. Their weaker companions remained inert in their beds, snoring, dribbling and groaning as high-proof sweat seeped slowly from their pores. The fortunate ones were still unconscious, their brains adrift in a liquid limbo, but others had woken to the full panoply of midget marching bands, pygmy panel-beaters and dwarfish dental drillers, all working overtime inside their skulls.

Willie and Cynthia had left the party at a respectable time and, when he returned to the Bothy next morning, Willie could only shake his head sadly.

"Aye" he sighed, prodding one of the inert mounds, "the pleasures of drink!"

The mound groaned. From its hidden depths a small voice cried piteously:

"Asp'rins! Asp'rins!"

"Aye, OK" Willie said, "ah'll get some from Cook."

Then he bent close to the heap and shouted "Ah don't suppose you want a couple o' well fried eggs an' a nice bit o' fat bacon?"

He smiled grimly at the muffled scream from deep inside the heap of blankets.

As Willie returned from the cookhouse, breakfasted and cheerfully rattling a large bottle of painkillers, Grallocher hove into view. Normally they would have ignored each other, but Grallocher appeared to change course. Willie slowed down and glowered as he approached.

"On an errand of mercy, MacBog? Florence bloody Nightingale, eh! Your wee pals not feeling so good?"

"Whit's it tae you, Grallocher?"

"Oh, nothing, nothing."

"Then whit'r ye jibberin' aboot?"

Grallocher did not reply, but grinned horribly and tapped the side of his nose.

"Piss off, Grallocher. Ah've scraped nicer things'n you off the sole o' ma boot."

Willie watched him go. There was a definite spring in Grallocher's step. As he reached the corner of the building he stopped and looked back, still grinning. Willie looked around for a rock to throw, but he was gone.

Willie sat in the Bothy, reflecting pensively. Why was Grallocher so cheerful? Grallocher was never cheerful. His thoughts were interrupted when Cynthia made a brief appearance, bearing tea and sympathy for the drink-racked remnants of the previous night's festivities. For all her gentle upbringing she bore up well in the face of the gruesome carnage of cans, bottles and bodies which still littered the Bothy. As she sat talking with Willie there was a rasping sound from behind the toilet door, a short silence, then a long, low groan. This was repeated several times. Obviously, even the gentle noise of the Inverdruel 'Bugle' being torn into strips was too much for someone's shattered nerve ends to bear. Then there was a loud thump, and a moan. A Beater had come unfurled from his blankets and fallen out of bed. Like the pallid contents of a sausage roll spilled from its pastry casing, the Beater lay on the hard floorboards, twitching and shivering.

Cynthia knelt down beside the trembling body.

"Asthrmans, asthrmans" it whispered through barely moving lips.

Cynthia looked up, a worried expression on her face.

"I think he's got asthma."

"Naw, naw" said Willie, "give 'im a few o' these", and he tossed over the bottle of aspirins.

CHAPTER 24

"So who's the bloody comedian, then?"

The Beaters looked up, each a picture of injured innocence.

Only minutes previously Willie had departed to pay his normal twilight visit to his beloved. Now he was back, and looking mighty peeved.

"Christ, Willie, that was quick! Wuz it wan o' they premature inoculations? Ah've read aboot them in the problem page o' 'The Bugle'."

The level of the alcoholic floodwaters swirling around the Beaters' skulls had dropped considerably through the course of the day and, although large numbers of brain-cells had been loosened from their moorings and swept away, never to be seen again, the Beaters' natural insouciance was swiftly reasserting itself. Willie had noticed this.

"Don't you fuckin' zombies start givin' me cheek!"

"So whit's yer problem, Willie?"

"Some basturd chained ma ladder to a four-by-two. An' the four-by-two is an integral fuckin' part o' the fuckin' shed! THAT's the fuckin' problem!"

The Beaters looked at one another. "So ye canny get up tae Cynthia's room?"

"Exactly!"

"Well, it wisnae us, big yin, honest!"

Willie stared out through the window at the darkness beyond. A hard, mean look crossed his face.

"Grallocher! The basturd! Ah've been sabotaged! That's why he wuz so bloody smarmy this mornin'. He'd a face on 'im like a constipation case that's jist won a hunnerweight o' prunes in a raffle. Basturd! Ah'll huv tae explain tae Cynthia in the mornin'. Even worse, ah'll huv tae stay wi' you lot tonight. Jist when ah wuz gettin' used tae better things, too!"

"We don' mind, Willie" said the connoisseur of 'The Bugle's' problem page, magnanimously.

"Jist so long as you don't try interferin' wi' oor libidos while we're sleepin'."

CHAPTER 25

Early the next morning Willie and Cynthia met, and wandered off, deep in conversation, down the path towards the stream. This had previously been a place of pleasant associations, where they could go alone, but now their footsteps were dogged by Grallocher's clammy shadow.

Back in the Bothy the Beaters sat around, some playing cards in desultory fashion. Their normal sparkle seemed to have deserted them. "That basturd Grallocher, eh. He's bound tae spill the beans aboot Willie 'n' Cynthia."

"Aye, he's jist bidin' his time."

"Ah'll bet he'll be off doon tae the hospital tae see the Major, an' his mooth'll be goin' like a bloody castanet."

"Christ, aye. The Major'll be lyin' there, his arse in plaster an' no' jist feelin' a hunner per cent, an' then ol' smarm-features'll come stompin' in wi' a bag o' grapes an' say "How're ye doin', Major? Jist thought ah'd mention it, by the way, McBog's knockin' off yer daughter."

"Naw, he widnae be as tactful as that. He widnae bother wi' grapes."

Suddenly, outside the Bothy, footsteps scrunched, the door opened and Brent stooped and came in.

"Howdy, fellahs. Is Willie about?"

Willie appeared behind him.

"Aye, Brent, ma man. Saw ye headin' over. How's it goin'?"

"Things ain't lookin' too hot Willie. Ah've some bad news fer you, boy."

He steered Willie across to a corner, and they spoke in low, urgent tones. The Beaters watched anxiously.

"Aye, well, thanks Brent. Ye're a real gent."

Brent patted Willie's shoulder, then headed out of the Bothy and back to the House. Willie stood, chewing his bottom lip pensively.

"C'moan, Willie. Whit's the crack?

Well, boys" he said, "apparently oor ol' friend Grallocher is heid honcho while the Major's laid up in the hospital an', accordin' to Brent, he's took it oan himsel' tae issue the Guests wi' heavy-duty cartridges fur today's shoot."

The Beaters stared, aghast. Before they could say anything Willie held up his hand.

"You lot, go'n get yer breakfast. Ah'll huv tae go an' see Cynth."

"But Willie ... "

"Oot!"

They shuffled slowly out, muttering unhappily. A few minutes later Willie joined them in the cookhouse. He went over to Cook and spoke to her. She looked upset, then turned away, shaking her head slowly. The Beaters sullenly toyed with their porridge and glared at Willie mutinously.

"It's no' fair, Willie, whit aboot our agreements?"

"Aye, oor 'terms o' employment'."

"We're no' trained fur kamikaze work, ye know."

"Lead's bad fur ye. Gives ye brain damage."

"So does drink" growled Willie, "but that didnae stop ye swimmin' in it a couple o' nights back! Anyway, everythin's under control, jist trust me, boys."

"Urr ye sure, Willie?"

"Aye, ah'm sure."

"So we're no' goin' tae get oor arses shot full a' holes? Is that a promise?"

"Aye - it's a promise. Now eat yer fuckin' porridge, or ye'll upset Cook."

Cook had her back to the Beaters. She was slowly working her ladle backwards and forwards in the remnants of the porridge at the bottom of the cauldron. She did not want the boys to see her face.

A skein of geese passed high above, heading south, their forlorn honking still audible long after they had disappeared. The Beaters sat, packed together in the trailer, puffing nervously on their cigarettes and hunched against the chill wind which carried with it the first imperceptible whisper of approaching winter.

The Guests began to emerge from the House. Brent waved across cheerily. Then Grallocher appeared. He came across, a smirk flitting over his unsavoury features and, ignoring the looks of malevolent hatred from the Beaters, he climbed into the Land Rover and started it up.

As they jolted along the track, Willie and the Beaters huddled in conversation.

"Ah've got tae level wi' ye, boys. It's nippy sweetie time."

"You tellt us we'd no' get shot!"

"Naw, naw, wheesht, boys, yer safe enough, ah'll make sure o' that. Naw, it's me'n Cynth, we've bin talkin' this over, ye know, fur a while. It's the end o' the line, one way or the other. Once the Major finds oot, we're history. An', besides, there's mair complications'n you boys know aboot. So ... we've come tae a decision ... "

By the time they rumbled to a halt near the top of the hill the Beaters were still subdued, but their earlier mood of apprehension had lifted.

They clambered out of the trailer and stretched. Grallocher jumped down and slammed the door.

"Right, McBog" he said, his eyes shining with barely-suppressed excitement, "after the unfortunate accident on the hill last week the Major is not in a fit state to be with us today, so - *I* am in charge. I'll be going over now to assist the Guests. When you hear the whistle - well, you know the score, don't you, McBog?"

"Oh, aye" said Willie, slowly, "ah know the score."

Grallocher flashed a sudden, suspicious glance at Willie, then turned away abruptly and hauled himself into the Land Rover. The Beaters watched as it bounced away across the hill towards the assembled Guests.

pee ... ee ... eee

The whistle shrilled in the distance.

Jostling and pushing, the Beaters scampered up the slope. They crested the rise and came into view of the shooters.

"OK, boys" said Willie, "ah think evasive manoeuvres urr now called for", and they veered sharply away from the Guests, running hard.

"That'll do, boys" shouted Willie, and the Beaters slowed and turned, and began to run parallel to the guns. They heard the bang of several shots, but only intermittently, not the usual fusillade - the shooters were obviously confused. And that familiar roaring in the distance? The Beaters chortled with delight.

"He's gonny huv a fuckin' heart attack!"

Secure in the knowledge that they were just beyond effective range of the guns, the Beaters pulled out all the stops. They pranced along the skyline in full view of the shooters, mincing, blowing kisses, waving cheerfully. Several pretended to be shot, tumbling acrobatically into the heather, but spoiling the effect by repeating the process several times.

"OK, boys" said Willie, when the shooting had completely stopped, "ye've had yer fun, let's get oor arses back tae base camp."

As they trotted back to their starting point Grallocher's Land Rover appeared in the distance, bouncing violently over the tussocks and hollows. The Beaters stood around the trailer, watching as it approached. As it rumbled up and shuddered to a halt in front of them they instinctively shuffled closer together and made sure they were standing behind Willie. The door swung open with a crash, and Grallocher leapt out.

"You torn-faced wee hoors!"

His face was crimson and his eyes bulged as he rushed towards them, arms flailing.

Willie took one step forward. There was a sickening crack as Grallocher's nose broke.

CHAPTER 26

When the Land Rover and trailer roared up to the Bothy Cynthia was already waiting at the door, a suitcase beside her. Willie jumped down.

"Alive'n well, doll, alive'n well. Will you be needin' a chauffeur, missis?"

They grinned at each other.

"You little basturds" he roared at the Beaters, "get that trailer off, pronto!"

"Ah'll jist be a minute", and he dashed round the corner towards the canteen. He returned with Cook. The Beaters stood around, looking sheepish.

"OK, Cynth, in ye get."

Cynthia climbed in and slid open the window.

"Thanks for everything, boys" she said, "I love you all", and she blew the Beaters a kiss. They shuffled with embarrassment.

"Aye. We'll be seein' you."

Willie planted a kiss on Cook's rosy cheek. She smiled, but her eyes were bright with tears. He hauled himself into the driver's seat, turned the key and the engine roared into life.

"Give ma regards tae Brent!" he shouted above the noise.

The Beaters stood and watched as the Land Rover rumbled slowly off down the drive. Willie hung from the window.

"Ah'll catch you basturds in the big smoke. Behave yersel's now!"

And, gathering speed, the Land Rover passed through the trees and out of sight.

As they dipped down into the dark shadow of Glendruel Cynthia stared out at the desolate landscape and shivered. But then, in the warmth of the Land Rover, hearing the familiar growl of the engine, and with Willie beside her, she felt reassured. She glanced across. He was bent over the wheel, concentrating on the road. She turned away and stared out of the window, smiling to herself.

"If it's a boy" she thought, "we'll call it William."

High above, almost out of sight, two buzzards squealed and tumbled in the steel-blue sky.

CHAPTER 27

Jimmy trudged homewards, through the dark, deserted streets. Drizzle flecks flickered in the street lamps' staggered orange orbits. He hunched over his bag of chips, feeling the vinegary heat in his stomach spreading through his chilled body. His cagoule had long since ceased to be waterproof.

"Geeza chip, ya wee basturd!"

He looked up. There were three of them, cutting swiftly across the street towards him. Jimmy waited, numbly resigned to his fate.

"Geeza chip then!"

"Gaw'n fuck yersel."

They looked down at him with hard, pitiless stares. One of them suddenly sniggered,

"Ach, leave the wee shite. Ye canny go hittin' midgets!"

Their raucous laughter echoed as they went on their way.

"Jesus fuckin' Christ! Ah'm no' even worth a boot in the arse!" and, in a sudden spasm of rage and despair, Jimmy hurled his chips to the ground.

At the end of the street he turned and looked back. It was deserted, apart from a skinny dog which had slunk from a nearby close and was furtively wolfing down his chips.

"YA BUNCH A' SHITES!"

He turned and trudged towards the high-rise flats which loomed beyond the surrounding houses. He was totally pissed off. Ever since he had been turned down for a job by Stratford Hathaway, on the grounds of restricted growth, the sweetie jar of life had dealt him nothing but fistfuls of hard centres. He had lost all contact with the other Beaters and now the days slipped away in a haze of alcoholic boredom or were spent staring glassy-eyed at television soaps, children's programmes and game-shows. The final straw had been the death of his gerbils. The little bastards had gone and croaked within a week of each other. Their ping-pong ball helmets still sat on the sideboard.

He let himself into the flat. At the far end of the corridor he saw his mother through the open kitchen door. She was bent over the frying pan, a fag-end in the corner of her mouth, her support-stockings sagging round her ankles.

"Zat you Jimmy?"

"Aye, maw."

"Yer tea's oan."

"It's OK, maw, ah'm no' hungry."

"Ach well, mair for the auld yin."

Jimmy dropped into the armchair. 'Baywatch' was on. He liked 'Baywatch'. There was some good acting on 'Baywatch'. And wimmen. Lots of wimmen. He heard the outside door open.

"Zat you Jimmy?"

"Aye."

"Yer tea's oan."

"OK."

A small figure appeared in the doorway. Jimmy senior wore an ankle-length overcoat and a flat cap, and was holding a plastic bag full of beer-cans. He unbuttoned his coat and hung it in the hallway, then came into the room. He looked slightly ridiculous in his wellington boots and crimson tights, and the short silver cape, scorched slightly round the edges, and the flat cap were not really an ensemble.

"Another basturd o' a day" he sighed, "missed the net twice."

Jimmy senior had just completed another day on the Government Training Scheme for the Long Term Unemployed. As part of his Personal Development Programme he was undergoing a course in circus skills. It was that or lose his benefit. Perhaps because of his diminutive stature he had been allocated to the Human Cannonball section.

He flicked his silver cape out from behind him and sank into a chair.

"Here ye go, son" he said, passing over a can of lager, "get yer tonsils roon' that."

"Ah've been thinkin', da."

Jimmy senior spluttered and almost choked on a mouthful of beer. Wiping foam from his mouth with the back of his hand, he peered anxiously at his son.

"Ah'm gonny fuck off."

"Aye?"

"Aye, back up north. Fur ol' times' sake, ye know."

"Ach, but there's nothin' there noo, son. It's bin two years. An' yer ol' mates frae Inverdruel, gawd knows where they are noo."

"Aye, but there's no' a lot doin' here, is there? Ah jist want tae huv a wee tramp aboot the old haunts, ye know. Whit dae ye think?"

"Hmm ... anither can o' beer?"

CHAPTER 28

Jimmy stepped off the train. He gazed around, inhaling deeply. Bloody magic! He had forgotten what fresh air smelled like.

"Well" he thought, "furst step is tae check oot the ol' waterin' hole!"

And hefting his rucksack onto his shoulder he strode off out of the station. He made his way up the main street. Nothing much seemed to have changed. A few passers-by stared, then gave him slight nods of recognition. When he reached the square he dropped his rucksack at his feet and gazed at the Hotel. He shook his head slowly, old memories flooding back.

"Aye, wild nights in there, right enough. Them were the days."

After a few moments' contemplation he reached down for his bag and humphed it onto his shoulder.

"Well" he thought, "ah suppose they still sell beer", and he went up to the Hotel and pushed open the bar door.

Two toddlers sat facing each other in the middle of the floor. The little boy looked apprehensive. Well he might. Suddenly the little girl's fist shot out and she poked him in the eye with the soggy end of a half-chewed rusk. In her other hand she held a plastic feeding-bottle by the teat, and in a flash she swung it round in an arc and caught him a solid blow on the side of the head. As the little boy put his hands up, one over his eye and one to his ear, a small podgy fist sailed into his face, and he began to blubber loudly.

"Aphradite! Leave young William alone! Ah won't tell you again!"

Jimmy stared across in the direction of the voice. For a few moments, apart from a muffled snuffling noise from the small boy in the middle of the floor, there was total silence ...

"Andromeda! ... Willie! ... Cynthia! ... Ally? ... Allo?"

"Aloysius. An' if it's not yersel' bejasus! The smallest Beater that ever tramped the hill!"

"How're ye doin', ya wee basturd!" said Willie, coming over and giving Jimmy a delighted slap on the ear.

"Great tae see ye, wee man! Long time, eh! Park yer arse, park yer arse! Andromeda! Pint fur the wee man here!"

As the afternoon slowly dissolved into a golden alcoholic haze Jimmy was brought up to date with all the events of the last couple of years. In between pints he learned that, after Willie and Cynthia's departure from Inverdruel, Aloysius and Andromeda's relationship had burgeoned, and the result of their union, Aphradite, had young William in a head-lock at that particular moment. Aloysius, never a man to do things by halves, and enthralled by Andromeda's muscular charm, had sold up his various enterprises in Ireland and purchased Inverdruel Hotel. Meanwhile, deprived of its regular Beaters, Glendruel Estate was hardly viable and Aloysius's keen nose for a bargain led to his making Major Manley-Buttocks a modest financial offer which he was given exactly one week to decide on. The Major and Maud now resided in a home for distressed gentle-folk, on the south coast of England.

Aloysius had big plans for the estate. The two acres of lucky white heather were coming on well, and his major investment, apart from buying out Manley-Buttocks, the conversion of Glendruel House into the Glendruel Executive Training and Assessment Centre, was already starting to produce financial returns. Co-opting Brent Crude onto the board of Glendruel Enterprises plc was the sort of move that had "Aloysius Flannelly" stamped all over it. Young, thrusting executives from large companies and corporations (many from the world of oil) were sent to Glendruel for week-long courses. There they were subjected to all manner of physical and mental hardships in order to assess them for initiative, teamwork and leadership qualities. They would be loaded into a trailer and towed at speed over rough tracks. Then, out in the hills, they were forced to run through heather and bogs while being constantly subjected to a barrage of verbal and sometimes physical abuse. The Course Instructors were almost entirely drawn from the ranks of ex-Beaters. It had taken all Aloysius's powers of persuasion to convince Andromeda that Willie would be the best person for the job of Chief Instructor, but she had finally come round.

The ex-Beaters, of course, knew the ground intimately and had a range of vocabulary which stretched the thrusting young executives to the limit. When the executives were trailered back, numb and exhausted, to the Glendruel Assessment Centre at the end of each day, they were then supplied with extremely basic food in spartan conditions. Cook got really upset if they did not leave their plates spotless.

"Right, you two, you've had enough. Here's Cynthia wi' yer transport."

Aloysius helped Andromeda to assist first Willie, then Jimmy, out of the bar and get them levered into the back of the company Land Rover.

"There ye go, Cynth" said Aloysius, "there's a couple a' lads for the casualty unit, right enough."

"Ah, I'll not be too hard on them this time" said Cynthia, "a couple of well-fried eggs and some nice fatty bacon for breakfast, perhaps."

"Don't worry about young William" said Andromeda, "we'll bring him over later. I think Aphradite wants to play with him a bit longer." The Land Rover moved slowly off. As it rumbled towards the bottom end of Inverdruel's main street, two figures stumbled out of Ali Mahindra's off-licence. One opened a plastic carrier-bag and they both peered in as if checking the contents then, apparently satisfied, they lurched off unsteadily down the road. An old dog hirpled slowly along some distance behind them, a length of knotted string trailing from its collar. One of the figures stopped and looked back.

"C'mon y' shtupit an'mal" urged Doctor McLush in slurred tones, "hav'n got ... all day."

"Yesh" agreed Grallocher, hiccuping and squinting back at the dog through bloodshot eyes, "shtup't an'mal. Hav'n got ... all day ... y'know!"

Jim plodded steadily along. He did not mind a spot of invective. That nice Mr Mahindra had given him a bhaji. It was far too precious to eat immediately. He was going to take it home and bury it.

Lightning Source UK Ltd.
Milton Keynes UK
27 August 2009

143143UK00001BA/2/P